Cyrus Jeffries

The Doctrine of the Judgment

Cyrus Jeffries

The Doctrine of the Judgment

ISBN/EAN: 9783337565053

Printed in Europe, USA, Canada, Australia, Japan

Cover: Foto ©Andreas Hilbeck / pixelio.de

More available books at **www.hansebooks.com**

THE
DOCTRINE OF THE JUDGMENT

AS REVEALED IN THE

SCRIPTURES OF DIVINE TRUTH:

IN WHICH IT IS SHOWN THAT THE GOSPEL DAY IS

THE JUDGMENT DAY,

AND THAT MANKIND ARE ALL TRIED IN THIS LIFE, AND

RECEIVE THE AWARD OF THE JUDGMENT

IMMEDIATELY AFTER DEATH;

AND ARE ASSIGNED TO

HEAVEN OR HELL,

ACCORDING TO THE DEEDS DONE IN THE BODY ON EARTH.

"AND JESUS SAID, FOR JUDGMENT I AM COME INTO THE
WORLD."—*John*, ix: 39.

By CYRUS JEFFRIES,
MINISTER OF THE GOSPEL IN THE CHURCH OF CHRIST
IN AMERICA.

———————·———————

LANCASTER, PA:
INQUIRER BUILDING, NORTH QUEEN STREET.
1868.

TO

THE MEMBERS

OF

THE CHURCH OF CHRIST IN AMERICA,

IS THIS WORK RESPECTFULLY INSCRIBED.

As the design of the author, in these pages, is, if possible, to give a clearer view of the Bible doctrine of the Judgment than any he has yet noticed in the teachings on theology, as well as to show the perfect rectitude of the Supreme Judge of the world in his decisions of human destiny, he trusts that his labors will not be in vain, and he feels that if this little book will do nothing more than merely lead its readers to a more thorough examination of the Bible, he will have accomplished his object.

May you all receive a crown of righteousness at the judgment-seat of Christ,

Is the prayer of your brother in the Gospel,

CYRUS JEFFRIES.

PREFACE.

Seeing that it was contrary to the opinion of civilized mankind to condemn any intelligent being to punishment without trial and judgment, I saw that it was much more contrary to the rectitude of the Supreme Judge of the World to send men to hell before they are judged and found guilty, or to send men to Heaven before they are judged and found worthy. And seeing that the doctrine of a general judgment at the end of the world must send all the wicked to hell before they are judged and found guilty, and all the righteous to heaven before they are judged and found worthy, and that the wicked must remain in hell, and the righteous in Heaven, for thousands of years or until the judgment, before they can be brought out of hell and out of heaven for trial, and that the wicked could only be tried and sent back to hell again as they were before, and the righteous, also, could only be tried and sent back again to heaven as they were before the judgment; and believing that this is not only contrary to reason, but to all the laws of God concerning the destiny of man, and seeing that it was the doctrine of a general judgment at the end of the world that forced the Roman Catholic Church to adopt the idea of a purgatory, or middle state for the dead, and that it was the idea of a future and general judgment that forced some of the orthodox churches to adopt the doctrine of an intermediate state of the dead, and others to adopt the doctrine of the sleep of the soul between death and the judgment—and then turning to the Scriptures of Divine Truth, and giving them a careful and prayerful examination, I found that mankind are all on trial here on earth, and are being judged as they pass along, for all the thoughts, words and actions of their lives, and that they receive the final judgment and award, immediately after death, at the judgment seat of Christ, in the spirit world, where the wicked are found guilty and sent away into everlasting punishment, and where the righteous are found worthy and received into life eternal; so that every wicked soul is tried and judged before it is sent to hell, and every righteous soul is tried and judged before it is received into glory. As no man, in justice, can be punished until

he is found guilty here on earth, much less would the Supreme Judge
of the world send the souls of the sons and daughters of men to be
punished in hell before they were tried, and judged, and found guilty
of transgression deserving of hell punishment.   But if the wicked go
to hell when they die, and the judgment is not until the end of the
world, then the wicked are punished before they are judged, and are
sent into torment before they are found guilty and deserving of punishment ; which dreadful doctrine is not only contrary to the jurisprudence of enlightened mankind, but to all the teachings of the
word of God, as shown in the following pages.   The Scriptures of
Divine Truth teach us that the Gospel day is the judgment day, and
that the judgment is now going on among men ; that all are being
judged as they pass along in life, and that every one feels and knows,
in his own heart, the decision of the judgment on his every action.
If he does a good action for the benefit of man or the glory of God,
he feels the justifying influence of the judgment, and has peace of
mind the moment he has performed the action.   But if he does a bad
action for the injury of man and the desecration of the character of
God, he feels the condemning influence of the judgment the moment
he has committed the action, and a state of unrest and sadness fills
his heart with forebodings of evil and unhappiness every time his
mind recurs to the commission of the action ; unless, through great
wickedness, his conscience has become seared as with a hot iron, and
he feels no more condemnation for sin.   Thus, the Gospel day is the
judgment day, and all mankind are tried as they pass along through
life, and, at death, receive the final judgment that lifts the righteous
to everlasting life and consigns the wicked to everlasting misery, according to their actions done on earth.   May every reader of these
pages so live, that when they come to die, they may be ready to appear before the judgment seat of Christ, in the spirit world, and receive a crown of righteousness at his right hand in the Paradise of
God.   THE AUTHOR.

THE
DOCTRINES OF THE JUDGMENT;
AS REVEALED IN THE
SCRIPTURES OF DIVINE TRUTH.

THE DOCTRINES.

Now is the Judgment of this world; for Christ came into the world for Judgment, and this being the day of salvation, it is, therefore, the day of Judgment. The Gospel day is the Judgment day; for Judgment is come upon all men, either to condemnation or justification of life, so that the Judgment is now going on, and men are being Judged for the deeds done in the body as they pass along in life, and, at death, receive the final Judgment which consigns them to endless happiness or misery, according to their works in time and earth.

"And I saw another angel fly in the midst of heaven, having the everlasting gospel to preach unto them that dwell on the earth, and to every nation, and kindred, and tongue, and people; saying with a loud voice, Fear God, and give glory to him; for the hour of his judgment is come; and worship him that made heaven, and earth, and the sea, and the fountains of waters."—*Rev.* xiv: 6—7.

The preaching of the gospel, by the angel that John saw flying in the midst of Heaven, was the ushering in of the gospel dispensation at the end of the Jewish age, when Christ set up his spiritual kingdom on earth, and the law of carnal rights and ceremonies, with all its types and shadows, was taken out of the way and the kingdom of the everlasting gospel established among men, that every nation, kindred, tongue and people might not only hear the tidings of salvation, but that they should have with it the judgment of the Redeemer, to show them their justification or their condemnation, according to their works, as they pass along in time. The angel, who had the gospel to preach to all people, declared with a loud voice: "*Fear God and give glory to him; for the hour of his judgment* IS COME;" which shows us that the gospel and the judgment both came together; so that the gospel day is the judgment day. For in the hour that the angel announced the beginning of the preaching of the gospel to the nations, in that same hour he announced the beginning of his judgment, that all men might know their reception or rejection of God; and his judgment will either approve or condemn them, according to their actions in life and time; which shows us, plainly, that the day of the gospel is the day of judgment, and that all are judged as they pass through life; and that, at death, they will receive the final sentence of the Judge, who will assign the righteous to everlasting life in the realms of joy, and the wicked to everlasting death in the regions of woe.

" Now is the judgment of this world: now shall the prince of this world be cast out."—*John*, xii: 31

The world has long been taught, by the commandments of men, that the judgment is not to take place until the end of time, or at the end of the world. But Christ says "*now is the judgment of this world; now* shall the prince of this world be cast out." The judgment is now going on, and men are judged for their good or bad actions as they are committed. And when the evil spirit, or prince of this world, is cast out of the heart by the gospel or spirit of Christ, and the man becomes truly converted to God, he is adjudged righteous, and enters on the journey of his immortality. But the wicked remain under the influence of the spirit of evil, or the prince of this world, and, consequently, are under the judgment of condemnation, and will be lost forever unless they repent and turn to God. For now is the judgment of this world by Christ, who will give to every man, at death, his reward; to the righteous, a home in heaven with the saved, and to the wicked, a home in hell with the lost.

" Therefore, as by the offence of one judgment came upon all men to condemnation, even so by the righteousness of one the free gift came upon all men unto justification of life."—*Rom.*, v : 18.

The first Adam brought sin into the world, but, under the promise and in the fullness of time, the second Adam, who is Christ, our Lord, brought righteousness by his gospel, and as righteousness and sin are the two great opposing elements for the salvation or the destruction of mankind, in time and to all eternity, and as mankind are now on trial and in a state of probation under these two great influences, righteousness and sin, it is evident that judgment must be executed upon the sons and daughters of men, according to their actions, as they pass along in time, and that we are now standing at the bar of trial in this, the judgment or gospel day, else we could not receive the free gift or pardon unto justification of life; nor could judgment be upon all men to condemnation, if it were not now here, going on; so that all who believe and, by their actions, obey Christ, are judged and justified before him in this life, and all who, by their actions, reject and disobey Christ, are judged and condemned before him.

"Because he hath appointed a day, in the which he will judge the world in righteousness, by that man whom he hath ordained: whereof he hath given assurance unto all men, in that hath raised him from the dead."—*Acts*, xvii: 31.

This day, which is the day of salvation, or the gospel day, had long been appointed. It began at the second coming of Christ, when he set up his spiritual kingdom at the destruction of Jerusalem, which was the beginning of the gospel day, or judgment day—the day in which we now live, and the day in which Christ is judging the world; and it is the last day, for there is no day of human probation beyond the gospel day. Men must be tried and judged for their actions in this life, and receive their final sentence at death, or they could not be sent to their respective places of happiness or woe, as their good or bad life demands. This is the reason why God has appointed a day, which is the gospel day, in the which he will judge the world by that man whom he hath ordained, our blessed Lord and Savior, Jesus Christ. For if men are not judged until the end of the world, then they are sentenced before they are judged; for the wicked, at death, are sent to their eternal home in hell, and the righteous, at death, to their eternal home in heaven; so that the states of both the wicked and the righteous are fixed forever in the eternal world, and no judgment, hereafter, can ever alter or change the condition of the saved or lost in the spirit world. All that a general judgment could do, would be to bring the righteous out of heaven and the wicked out of hell, judge them, and send them back again into their respective conditions. But even to do this, would be to disturb the harmony of heaven and the happiness of the saints. For what righteous spirit could look upon the distorted features or listen to the agonizing cries of the lost millions on the left hand of the Judge without pain and horror, especially if they beheld their own kindred among the damned? But when we behold the countless millions of the heavenly host, thus situated in relation to their parents, husbands, wives and children, who, with blazing hands and screaming tongues, implore their help as they sink back to hell, would it not cause a pang of horror to thrill through all the ranks of Heaven that would disturb and fill with unrest the angel world forever?

"But now once in the end of the world hath he appeared to put away sin by the sacrifice of himself. And as it is appointed unto men once to die, but after this the judgment: so Christ was once offered to bear the sins of many; and unto them that look for him shall he appear the second time without sin unto salvation."—*Heb.*, ix: 26—28.

"But now once in the end of the world hath he appeared to put away sin by the sacrifice of himself." The end of the world is the end of the ages, or the end of all the dispensations allotted to man until the coming of Christ, at the end of the Jewish economy, and the beginning of those last days by which the holy prophets represented the then distant gospel dispensation, or gospel day, which was ushered in by the coming of our Lord and Savior, to put away sin by the sacrifice of himself; after which, he arose from the dead, appeared unto his disciples, commissioned them to preach his gospel to every creature, and, under the glorious promise of his second coming, in his spiritual kingdom, ascended to glory; and after preparing a place for his people, he descended and took away the old covenant, which he had fulfilled, destroyed Jerusalem and its Jewish temple worship, and set up his spiritual kingdom, which was not only the end of the world, or of the ages, but the beginning of his spiritual reign, which is the gospel day, or the day of judgment.

"And as it is appointed unto men once to die, but after this the judgment." By Adam's transgression, all men were appointed to death, both natural and moral, and as Christ did not come to save men from natural death, He, of course, came to save them from endless death; and in order to effect this, the Son of God had to first resurrect them from the death of trespass and sin into the gospel kingdom, or last dispensation of God to man on earth, or the gospel day, which is the judgment day, or the day in which Christ set up his judgment in the earth; for "He shall not fail nor be discouraged, till He have set judgment in the earth," (*Isa.*, xlii: 4,) which was done when the spiritual kingdom of the gospel was established at the second coming of Christ, and is now going on; so that all men are acquitted or condemned as they pass along, until death, when the final judgment, pronounced by Christ, the righteous Judge, assigns them to their eternal destiny; they that have done righteously, to everlasting joy, and they that have done wickedly, to everlasting woe.

"It is appointed unto men once to die, but after this the judgment." Every one, as soon as he leaves the body at death, goes directly to the judgment seat of Christ, the Supreme Judge of the world, where he will receive the final verdict: to either live in everlasting bliss, or dwell in misery forever. Like Lazarus, the righteous, at death and final judgment, will be borne to the Paradise of God, where they will increase in happiness, wisdom and glory forever; while the wicked, like the rich man, at death and the final judgment, will be borne to the Hades of the damned, where they shall be punished with sorrow, anguish and horror for ever and ever.

"So Christ was once offered to bear the sins of many, and unto them that look for him shall he appear the second time without sin unto salvation." As Christ had come the first time, and was made an offering for the sins of the world, that mankind might be redeemed from under the curse of original transgression, and the law fulfilled in their stead by the Son of God, so was he to appear the second time, without sin unto salvation. He was not to appear the second time unto the destruction of the world, but unto salvation; that is, to set up his spiritual kingdom and establish the gospel of salvation on earth; which he did, according to his promise, when he ended all the ceremonies, types and shadows of the Jewish economy, fulfilled the symbols, signs and emblems of his second advent, destroyed Jerusalem with its temple and its offerings, and filled the world with the glory of his gospel. They that were looking for him to come the second time were his apostles, disciples and all true believers, for "He" had "said unto them, verily I say unto you, That there be some of them that stand here which shall not taste of death, till they have seen the kingdom of God come with power" (*Mark*, ix: 1);

and that "Ye shall not have gone over the cities of Israel, till the Son of Man be come," (*Matt.*, x: 23.) And again, "I tell you of a truth, there be some standing here which shall not taste of death till they see the kingdom of God," (*Luke*, ix: 27.) And again, the Savior said, "Verily I say unto you, There be some standing here, which shall not taste of death, till they see the Son of Man coming in his kingdom," (*Matt.*, xvi: 28.) As the Savior had already come once, this, of course, was his second coming. And it was not to be a coming of wrath to burn the material world of man, but a coming of salvation to man. His first coming was in the flesh, but his second coming was in the spirit, by which he brought in the day of salvation, which is the gospel day, or judgment day. For all admit the second coming of Christ is the great day— the day for which all other days were made, the judgment day, which is the day of salvation.

"But the heavens and the earth, which are now, by the same word, kept in store, reserved unto fire against the day of judgment and perdition of ungodly men. But, beloved, be not ignorant of this one thing, that one day is with the Lord as a thousand years, and a thousand years as one day."—II *Peter*, iii: 7—8.

The heavens and the earth, mentioned in this Scripture, were the Jewish Church and State, which were kept in store through all the fall of thrones, the wreck of nations and the ruin of empires; reserved unto fire against the day of judgment and perdition of ungodly men; which was literally fulfilled at the destruction of Jerusalem, where the temple, that had continued just one day, or a thousand years, was also consumed with fire at the beginning of the day of Judgment. And the believers were cautioned not to be ignorant of this one thing: That one day, with the Lord, is as a thousand years, and a thousand years as one day; so that the day of judgment here spoken of is as a thousand years or dispensations; which shows, beyond all doubt, that the gospel day is the judgment day, and that the sons and daughters of men are now on trial, where they are being judged as they pass along, until death, immediately after which, they receive the great verdict of the judgment by the Supreme Judge of the world, who assigns them to heaven or hell, forever, according to their righteous or wicked lives on earth.

"For I am now ready to be offered, and the time of my departure is at hand. I have fought a good fight, I have finished my course, I have kept the faith: Henceforth there is laid up for me a crown of righteousness, which the Lord, the righteous Judge, shall give me at that day; and not to me only, but unto all them also that love his appearing."—II *Tim.*, iv: 6—8.

The apostle Paul was now ready to die: the time of his departure was at hand; he was awaiting the axe of the executioner, who was to behead him in the presence of gazing thousands, in the great capitol of the world. But he had fought the good fight, he had finished his course, he had kept the faith; thenceforth there was laid up for him a crown of righteousness, which the Lord, the righteous Judge, would give him at that day, the day of his death; yes, the righteous Judge would judge him worthy of a crown of righteousness at that day—the day he finished his course, the day of his departure, the very day he died; for it is appointed unto men once to die, but after this the judgment. Christ, the righteous Judge, crowned him that day and assigned him a home of rapture and glory in the Paradise of God. The holy apostle did not have to wait until the end of time for the Judge to crown him, but he received his diadem of glory from the hand of the righteous Judge as soon as he left the natural body. And not unto him only shall a crown of righteousness and glory be given, but unto all them that love his appearing. O, may we all fight the good fight and keep the faith, so that when we have finished our course, and our departure is at hand, we may love to behold our Judge, when he appears at death, to decide our destiny, and that we may all receive a crown of righteousness at that day.

"I charge thee therefore before God, and the Lord Jesus Christ, who shall judge the quick and the dead at his appearing and his kingdom."—II *Tim.*, iv: 1.

The Lord-Jesus Christ is the Judge of the quick and the dead. The quick are the living, and are judged as they pass through life, according to the deeds they do in earth and time. The dead are those whose natural bodies die, and are judged or sentenced immediately after death, by the Lord Jesus Christ, to their respective destinies—the righteous to everlasting life and the wicked to everlasting death. His appearing and his kingdom was his second coming, when he set up his spiritual or gospel kingdom on earth, which was the beginning of the gospel day, or judgment day, in the world of man.

"Whoso keepeth the commandment shall feel no evil thing: and a wise man's heart discerneth both time and judgment. Because to every purpose there is time and judgment, therefore the misery of man is great upon him."—*Eccl.*, viii: 5—6.

They that keep the commandments of God shall feel no evil or judgment resting upon them, " because their hearts condemn them not and they have confidence toward God," who judgeth them righteously; for, being wise, they are able to discern both time and judgment, and that they, both alike, are going on, because to every purpose there is a time and judgment, so that the act and the judgment go together, or, rather, the judgment follows the act so closely that the misery of man is great upon him; he has not to wait until the end of the world for the judgment, for to every purpose there is time and judgment here on earth.

"Behold, the days come, saith the Lord, that I will raise unto David a righteous Branch, and a King shall reign and prosper, and shall execute judgment and justice in the earth."—*Jer.*, xxiii: 5.

This is the promise of the coming of Christ, who, through David's line, was to be a Prince and a Savior. At his first coming he was to redeem mankind from the bondage of sin and corruption, and at his second coming he was to set up his gospel kingdom, over which he was to reign and prosper, executing judgment and justice in the earth. And as Christ had come the second time, taken away the old, natural law, and established the new spiritual law in his gospel kingdom on the earth, it is evident that he is not only reigning, our God and King, but that he is now executing judgment and justice in the earth, and that the children of our race do not have to wait until the end of time for the fixing of their destiny by an imaginary judgment, but that they are judged as they move along the path of life, and receive, at death, the verdict that disposes of their case forever.

"For the Father judgeth no man; but hath committed all judgment unto the Son."—*John*, v: 22.

The Lord Jesus Christ being both God and man, is the only being in the Universe worthy and able to judge between God and man; therefore, all judgment is committed unto him. And as He is now reigning, the Supreme Judge of the world, it is evident that he is now judging the world, especially since he has declared that, "Now is the judgment of this world."

" And hath given him authority to execute judgment also, because he is the Son of Man."—*John*, v: 27.

He does not say he is going to give him authority to execute judgment at the end of the world, but that he *hath given* him already the authority to execute judgment also; which, observe, is in the present tense. "Because He is the Son of Man." Having lived in the flesh a man, subject, with all mankind, to the sorrows, temptations and trials of humanity, and being, at the same time, the true and Supreme Creator, he has fitted, as no other being in the Universe could be, to judge between the sons and daughters of Adam and their God. To judge as well as to redeem, and as redemption, judgment and the resurrection are the three great features of the gospel of Christ, and are all now going on in earth, it is, therefore, plain that the Son of God is now executing judgment in the world of man.

"Verily there is a reward for the righteous: verily he is a God that judgeth in the earth."—*Psa.*, lviii: 11.

In this we are clearly told that God judgeth in the earth; that his judgment is here and now, and that the righteous receive a reward as they journey along the path of time, which is the happiness of conscious rectitude, or the spiritual enjoyment they receive from God, the righteous Judge, who rewardeth them for the good actions they do in time; for "He is a God that judgeth in the earth."

"And he shall judge the world in righteousness, he shall minister judgment to the people in uprightness."—*Psa.*, ix: 8.

This not only shows us that the world is judged in righteousness, but that judgment is ministered to the people here on earth. Who, from reading these Scriptures, could suppose for a moment that the judgment is delayed until the end of time, when it is expressly said that judgment is ministered to the people.

"The just Lord is in the midst thereof: he will not do iniquity: every morning doth he bring his judgment to light, he faileth not." —*Zeph.*, iii: 5.

By this we are made to understand that the judgment of the Lord is going on day and night, for "every morning doth he bring his judgment to light, he faileth not."

"And Jesus said: For judgment I am come into this world: that they which see not might see, and that they which see, might be made blind."—*John*, ix: 39.

In this Scripture, the blessed Redeemer has plainly told us what he has come into this world for. No man need be mistaken here, for Jesus says: "For judgment I am come into this world," and if he has come into this world for judgment, (and all must admit that he is the Supreme Judge of the world,) then why should it be taught that the judgment is put off until the end of time? For his judgment is to make men, who are blind in ignorance, superstition and sin, to see the true and living way to everlasting life, and to make those blind who would see nothing but themselves and their own righteousness. For his judgment is ever with us, either justifying or condemning us in every action in life; and this is the reason why our great Judge has said, "For judgment am I come into this world."

"And if ye call on the Father, who without respect of persons judgeth according to every man's work, pass the time of your sojourning here in fear."—I *Peter*, i: 17.

Human language can make no plainer statement concerning the presence of the judgment than this. That while we are passing the the time of our sojourn here on earth, the Father "judgeth according to eveay man's work;" and that, too, without respect of persons. For he declares: "If ye call on the Father, who without respect of persons judgeth according to every man's work, pass the time of your sojourning here in fear."

"The Lord is known by the judgment which he executeth: the wicked is snared in the work of his own hands."—*Psa.*, ix: 16.

It is by the judgment that the Lord is known among men, from the fact that the wicked, sooner or later, are always snared in the work of their own hands. But how could the Lord be known by the judgment among men, if there was no judgment until the end of time? "But as the Lord is known by the judgment which he *executeth* now," it is every where evident that the judgment is now going on among the sons and daughters of men. Further, he "is known by the judgment which he executeth;" in this: that every person is conscious in their own minds of the approval or condemnation of the Supreme Judge the moment they commit an act, their very nature thus evidencing a present judgment.

"But when we are judged, we are chastened of the Lord, that we should not be condemned with the world."—I *Cor.*, xi: 32.

The judging of the righteous by the Lord, in this world, is the chastening of them for their sins, that there may be a deeper work of grace in the heart, a higher growth of righteousness in the soul, and a greater reformation in the character of his followers, that they may not be condemned with the world. But if the judgment is not to be until the end of the world, then this Scripture can have no meaning, for it declares that "when we are judged we are chastened of the Lord," which could not be at the last day, for the righteous go immediately into heaven, not to be chastened or chastized, but to be happy forever; so that it is here on earth where we are judged and chastened of the Lord.

"Be ye afraid of the sword: for wrath bringeth the punishments of the sword, that ye may know there is a judgment."—*Job*, xix: 28.

Wherever we see the sword destroying men and nations, we should know that it is the judgment of the Lord, and not that we should wait until the end of time for the judgment, for the punishments of the sword will not be known there. It is only here on earth, where the sword punishes, that we may know that the judgment is here on earth also.

"I scattered them among the heathen, and they were dispersed through the countries: according to their way and according to their doings I judged them.—*Eze.*, xxxvi: 19.

This shows us that the judgment is not only going on, but that the judgment of some is passed already, for the judgment, like redemption, extended backward as well as forward, to all the sons and daughters of men, and those who have been judged by the Supreme Judge of the world have been judged according to their doings. For he says: "According to their doings I judged them." And nowhere is it declared in the Book of God, that men have to wait until the end of time to be judged, but, on the contrary, it every where attests the divine truth that NOW is the judgment of this world.

"Grudge not one against another, brethren, lest ye be condemned: behold, the judge standeth before the door."—*James*, v: 9.

This not only shows us that the Judge standeth at the door of our hearts, judging every action there, but it shows us how carefully we should live, as the Judge is ever near us, and sees all the thoughts, intentions and actions of our hearts, and that he is ever judging the children of men, either condemning or acquitting them, according to their deeds.

"Behold my servant, whom I have chosen; my beloved, in whom my soul is well pleased: I will put my spirit upon him, and he shall shew judgment to the Gentiles."—*Matt.*, xii: 18.

This servant, or beloved One, was the long promised Redeemer, who was to come and show judgment to the Gentiles as well as to the Jews. The Gentiles were all the living nations, tribes, families and individuals of earth, who were not Jews, and, as they had never known anything of the judgment, Christ came to show them judgment, that they, through his suffering, death and resurrection, might not only know that the blessed Savior had shown salvation to the Gentiles, but that He had shown judgment to them, also, and has thereby proven to mankind that judgment is shown to the Gentiles before the end of time, and that it is not deferred until the end of the world, as some suppose.

" And also upon the servants and upon the handmaids in those days will I pour out my spirit. And I will shew wonders in the heavens and in the earth, blood, and fire, and pillars of smoke. The sun shall be turned into darkness, and the moon into blood, before the great and the terrible day of the Lord come."—*Joel*, ii : 29—31.

The pouring out of his spirit was the ushering in of his spiritual kingdom, or gospel day, for the gospel day is a spiritual dispensation. "The wonders in the heavens and the earth" were the signs that preceded the destruction of Jerusalem, or the second advent of Christ. "Blood, and fire, and pillars of smoke" were the dreadful wars and burnings in the destruction of Jerusalem. "The turning of the sun into darkness" was the obscuring of the infant church of Christ for a season, by the awful overthrow and desolation of the Jewish nationality. The turning of the "moon into blood" was the fulfilment and destruction of the Jewish church and economy. And "the great and the terrible day of the Lord" was the day of the gospel and the judgment, which is still going on, for the gospel day is the judgment day.

" And Enoch also, the seventh from Adam, prophesied of these. saying, Behold, the Lord cometh with ten thousand of his saints, To execute judgment upon all, and to convince all that are ungodly among them of their ungodly deeds which they have ungodly committed, and of all their hard speeches which ungodly sinners have spoken against him."—*Jude*, xiv : 15.

Enoch also prophesied of the gospel day, or the judgment day, when Christ should come in his spiritual kingdom, with the thousands of his saints, to execute judgment upon all, and to convince all that are ungodly among them. Now this is just what the gospel and the judgment is doing; for to convince is to persuade of the truth, and as this Scripture clearly declares that "The Lord cometh with ten thousand of his saints to execute judgment upon all and to convince all," or to persuade all of the truth of his gospel and of the heinousness of their ungodly deeds, and the hard speeches they have spoken against the Son of God while here in life and time, and therefore cannot be applied to a judgment at the end of the world, for then there would be none to convince or persuade, as the doom of all would be fixed forever. And further, to be convinced that the prophecy of Enoch refers to the second coming of Christ at the destruction of Jerusalem, we need only turn to other prophets. For as the setting up of the spiritual or gospel kingdom, together with its redemption, its judgment and its resurrection, was the most stupendous and august event that ever transpired on earth, for the present, future and eternal happiness of man, it is no wonder that it was first on the tongue of prophecy, and last on the lips of revelation. It was the event that mantled our orb with the splendors of salvation, and crowned the Son of God, the Jehovah of the Universe. And to confirm the prophecy of righteous Enoch, we will give the testimony of another holy prophet. "And the Lord my God shall come, and all the saints with thee. And it shall come to pass in that day, that the light shall not be clear, nor dark: But, it shall be one day, which shall be known to the Lord, not day, nor night: but it shall come to pass, that at evening time it shall be light. And it shall be in that day, that living waters shall go out from Jesusalem; half of them toward the former sea, and half of them toward the hinder sea: in summer and in winter shall it be. And the Lord shall be king over all the earth: in that day shall there be one Lord, and his name one."—(*Zac.* xiv: 5—9.) That this prophecy is a beautiful description of the coming in of the gospel kingdom, is the general opinion of the Christian world. "And the Lord my God shall come, and all the saints with thee." This is the general description given by the prophet of Christ setting up his spiritual kingdom, and bringing in the gospel or judgment day on earth; after which, he proceeds to give a particular description of that glorious and heavenly work, as follows: "And it shall come to pass in that day"— that day was the Jewish day, or the day of the Jewish church or temple worship—"that the light shall not be clear, nor dark." The Jewish doctrine, being part human and part divine, or partly natural and partly spiritual, was neither clear nor dark, but was of a twilight character. A day that stood between the night of heathen darkness and the day of gospel brightness, and was, therefore, neither clear nor dark. "But it shall be one day." As one day is as a thousand years, and a thousand years as one day, with the Almighty, some Jewish church stood just one day, or a thousand years; for it was just one thousand years from the time Solomon dedicated the temple until Christ came, which fulfils the prophecy that "it shall be one day." "Which shall be known to the Lord, not day, nor night." It was not to be a day composed of day and night. The day was, therefore, an age—the Jewish age. "But it shall come to pass, that at evening time it shall be light." This was the coming in of the gospel day that was to light the world with its glory. "And it shall be in that day that living waters shall go out from Jerusalem." These were the gospel waters of life and salvation, which were to flow to all nations, beginning at Jerusalem. "Half of them toward the former sea, and half of them toward the hinder sea." These waters flowed backward as well as forward. They went back unto Adam, as well as forward to the last child of his race. The gospel embraces the entire world of man. "In summer and in winter shall it be." Season, clime or country makes no difference in the gospel or it dispensation. It has heat for every heart, hues for every eye, and joys for every soul that will receive its heavenly boon. "And the Lord shall be king over all the earth." The gospel, or spiritual kingdom of Christ, embraces the whole world. The earth is the territory of the kingdom; mankind are the subjects; the gospel is the law, and Jesus Christ is the king, and this is the gospel or spiritual kingdom established by Christ at the end of the Jewish day or age. "In that day shall there be one Lord, and his name one." That day is the gospel day and the judgment day. The one Lord is the Lord Jesus Christ, who is the Supreme Judge of the world and God over all, and blessed forever more. And his name one, not three Gods in one, but three great essential principles in one person, who is the Jehovah, the Author and Owner of the Universe and all things therein. This is the One that Enoch prophesied of, when he said : Behold the Lord cometh with ten thousand of his saints, to execute judgment upon all and to convince all that are ungodly among them. Which is also corroborated by the apostle in his epistle to the Thessalonians, where he affirms the same truth, as follows: "To the end he may establish your hearts unblamable in holiness before God, even our Father, at the coming of our Lord Jesus Christ with all his saints." (*Thes.*, iii: 13.) Although the promise of the second coming of Christ, by the righteous Enoch, was more than three thousand years before the appearance of our blessed Savior in his kingdom, and that of the Apostle only about twenty-one years before the second advent of Christ, yet they both allude to the same great event, the second coming of Christ, and not to his first coming, as some have ventured to declare; for he did not come with all his saints at his first advent, nor will it be at the end of the world, as others have affirmed, for that would not be to establish their hearts unblamable in holiness before God. But it was that greatest of all events, the second coming of Christ, to set up his spiritual kingdom on earth, that Enoch and Paul spoke of, when they told of "The coming of our Lord Jesus Christ with all his saints." For this was the period when he took away the old covenant, abolished the Jewish church, destroyed their city and nationality, established his kingdom of salvation, erected the throne of his judgment, and opened up a new and living way, by which all the children of our race that will come, may come and be saved forever.

"Say among the heathen that the Lord reigneth: the world also shall be established that it shall not be moved: he shall judge the people righteously."—*Psa.*, xcvi: 10.*

This is the promise of the reign of our blessed Redeemer on earth. Then it was to be preached to the heathen that the Lord reigneth; that the world was to be established so that it should not be moved, when he came to judge the people righteously. Hence, it is plain that the judgment is before the end of the world; for it was only being established so that it could not be moved, when he should begin his reign, to judge the people righteously, and his reign began at the coming in of his spiritual kingdom, or the gospel day ; and as it is under this reign that he is to judge the people, it is evident that the gospel day is the judgment day.

"And as ye go, preach, saying, The kingdom of heaven is at hand."—*Matt.*, x: 7.

This is the command Christ gave to his ministers when he sent them forth to preach, which shows that the kingdom of heaven, or the spiritual kingdom, had not yet come, although Christ himself was here. Yet it was his first coming in which he was to suffer and to die in the flesh, for the redemption of

---

*This passage is treated in connection with the succeeding verses on page 37.

the world, that he might prepare it for the spiritual kingdom that was approaching, and which was the kingdom that the disciples were to preach was at hand. At his first coming, he came in the flesh, as a sufferer, to languish, bleed and die for the redemption of man ; at his second coming, he came in the spirit, as a king, to establish his kingdom for the happiness, equity and judgment of mankind on earth, and the salvation and glory of all who believe and obey, through all the enraptured ages of eternal life.

" Let the floods clap their hands : let the hills be joyful together before the Lord ; for he cometh to judge the earth : with righteousness shall he judge the world, and the people with equity."—*Psa.*, xcviii : 8—9.

This was the coming in of the gospel kingdom, when the world was to be made joyful at the second advent of Christ, when he came to judge the world with righteousness and the people with equity. For, at his first coming, he did not come to judge the world, and it could not be at the end of the world, for then there would be no floods and hills to clap their hands with joy, as the world, according to that view, with all its hills and floods, will be destroyed by the Judge. It can, therefore, only allude to the second coming of Christ, when he came to set up his kingdom and establish the gospel day, which is the judgment.

" Who shall give account to him that is ready to judge the quick and the dead. For, for this cause was the gospel preached also to them that are dead, that they might be judged according to men in the flesh, but live according to God in the spirit. But the end of all things is at hand : be ye therefore sober, and watch unto prayer." —I *Peter*, iv : 5—7.

All must give an account to him that is ready to judge the quick and the dead. Not *going to be ready* at the end of the world, but *is now ready*—now in life and time. The quick are the living, and the dead are the departed. He is ready to judge the quick, or the living, for all their actions as they pass along through life, and he is ready to give the verdict of that judgment at death, and assign each one to heaven or hell, according to their actions ; for " it is appointed unto men once to die, but after this the judgment." " For, for this cause was the gospel preached to them that are dead." These were the dead in trespasses and in sins. " That they might be judged according to men in the flesh." This shows us plainly that men *are judged* while they are in the flesh, and that they have not to wait until the end of the world to know whether they are to go to heaven or to hell, but that as soon as the natural body is dead, they go to either happiness or woe, according to the deeds done in the body. "But live according to God in the spirit." Since the second coming of Christ, all is spiritual. Men can no longer live after the flesh and be saved. They must live in the spirit, be led by the spirit, pray with the spirit, and worship God in the spirit, or they cannot be saved. They must, therefore, live according to God in the spirit. "But the end of all things is at hand; be ye therefore sober, and watch unto prayer." As the apostle wrote this just a little while before the coming of Christ and the end of the Jewish dispensation, it showed, of a truth, that the end of all things in the old religious world was at hand. In a very little time from that day, the Jewish rites and ceremonies would end. The types and shadows would end; the old covenant, with all its ordinances, would end; sacrifice and burnt offerings would end; the temple worship, with all its forms and symbols, would end; the Levitical priesthood, with all its solemn emblems, would end; the Hebrew Church and its economy would end; the Jewish government and empire would end; and even the great city Jerusalem, itself, would end, and the holy and spiritual kingdom of our blessed Lord and Savior, Jesus Christ, be established in their place. Truly, the end of all things was at hand, and, therefore, required every follower of the Savior, as it does now, to be sober, and to watch unto prayer.

"Behold my servant, whom I uphold; mine elect, in whom my soul delighteth; I have put my Spirit upon him : he shall bring forth judgment to the Gentiles."—*Isa.*, xlii : 1.

The elect One, in whom soul of God delighted, was the blessed Son of God, whose Spirit was put upon him that he might bring in the spiritual kingdom, and, with it, bring forth judgment to the Gentiles. He was not to bring judgment at the end of the world, but he was to bring it in when the Spirit of God was put upon him to establish his Church and kingdom on earth; then was he to bring forth judgment to the Gentiles. For the setting up of his gospel kingdom was the opening of the gospel day to the Gentile world; and the gospel day is the judgment day, or He would not have said that "He shall bring forth judgment to the Gentiles," at the same time he brought in his spiritual or gospel kingdom and reign on earth.

"He shall not fail nor be discouraged, till he have set judgment in the earth : and the isles shall wait for his law."—*Isa.*, xlii : 4.

This shows us plainly that Christ was not to fail until he had set his judgment in the earth. "And the isles were to wait for his law." Not only the continents of earth, but the islands of the sea, also, were to wait for the coming of his gospel or spiritual kingdom, when his law should extend over the world, and his judgment be set up or established in the earth.

"The Lord is in his holy temple, the Lord's throne is in heaven: his eyes behold, his eyelids try the children of men."—*Psa.*, xi : 4.

By this, we learn that the Lord is on his throne as the Supreme Judge of the world, where "his eyes behold, and his eyelids try the children of men;" which clearly shows us that mankind are not only before the throne of the Judge of all the earth, but that they are on trial, and are now being tried as they pass along in time; for life itself is but a state of probation or trial, at the close of which, the Supreme and ever righteous Judge awards to each their endless destiny, the righteous to everlasting life, and the wicked to everlasting death.

"Blessed is the man that endureth temptation : for when he is tried, he shall receive the crown of life, which the Lord hath promised to them that love him."—*James*, i : 12.

In our state of trial here on earth, it is a blessed thing to endure the temptations and the persecutions of the world, for when the great trial of life is terminated, and we have been tried before the spiritual bar of the Judge of all the earth, we shall receive a crown of life, which the Lord hath promised to them that love him. Hence, all men are tried in this life and receive their sentence at death, according to the deeds done in the body, whether they be good or evil.

"But, O Lord of hosts, that judgest righteously, that triest the reins and the heart, let me see thy vengeance on them : for unto thee have I revealed my cause."—*Jer.*, xi : 20.

The Lord is the righteous Judge that judgest righteously; not who is going to judge at the end of the world, but now, he is trying the hearts of the children of men. For the prophet knew that the Lord judged righteously and tried every heart truly, and that his own cause was before him, or he would not have asked the Lord to let him see his vengeance on the wicked.

" And when he is come, he will reprove the world of sin, and of righteousness, and of judgment."—*John*, xvi: 8.

Between the ascension and the second coming of Christ, the Holy Spirit, or Comforter, ministered to the Church of Christ, by reproving or convincing the world of sin, of righteousness and of judgment. That these three principles were in some sense existing is evident, or the Savior would not have told the disciples that "when He," the Comforter, "is come, he will reprove" or convince "the world of sin, and of righteousness, and of judgment." Righteousness and sin, or good and evil, were the two great contending principles for the eternal happiness or woe of the sons and daughters of men, and the judgment is the great discriminating principle of the Supreme Judge of the Universe, between right and wrong on earth, and the power to determine the state and destiny of the children of our race, according to the good or evil actions of their lives. It was now about being revealed to man, and was already exercised upon Satan, the prince of sin, in this world, as declared by the Savior in the eleventh verse : "Of judgment, because the prince of this world is judged," which shows us that Satan was already being judged, and the Holy Spirit was about to convince the world of the presence of the judgment on earth.

" For the time is come that judgment must begin at the house of God : and if it first begin at us, what shall the end be of them that obey not the gospel of God."—I *Peter*, iv : 17.

The time had come that judgment must begin at the house of God, or the Church of Christ on earth, and if the judgment began at the Church, when it was established in its spiritual glory by Christ on earth, why should it be taught that it is not to begin until the end of the world? This is too plain to be misunderstood. The apostle says: "For the time is come that judgment must begin at the house of God" or the Church, and not at the end of time, as taught by the creeds of men. O, how careful should we be to read and understand the Scriptures aright, that we may always be able to obey the gospel of Christ. For, "If it," the judgment, "first began at" the house of God, "what shall be the end of them that obey not the gospel of God?"

" But we are sure that the judgment of God is according to truth, against them which commit such things. And thinkest thou this, O man, that judgest them which do such things, and doest the same, that thou shalt escape the judgment of God? Or despisest thou the riches of his goodness, and forbearance, and long suffering: not

knowing that the goodness of God leadeth thee to repentance? But after thy hardness and impenitent heart, treasurest up unto thyself wrath against the day of wrath, and revelation of the righteous judgment of God; who will render to every man accordiug to his deeds."
—*Rom.*, ii : 2—6.

"But we are sure that the judgment of God IS according to truth." Not going to be according to truth at the end of the world, but IS NOW, at the present time, according to truth, "against them which commit such things." "And thinkest thou this, O man, that judgest them which do such things, and doest the same, that thou shalt escape the judgment of God?" Just as we judge our fellow men here and now, so will God judge us, and we cannot escape his judgment, for we are continually in his presence; he knows every thought, hears every word, and sees every action of our lives, and has no need to wait until the end of time to decide our destiny. "Or despisest thou the riches of his goodness, and forbearance, and longsuffering; not knowing that the goodness of God leadeth thee to repentance? But after thy hardness and impenitent heart, treasurest up unto thyself wrath against the day of wrath, and revelation of the righteous judgment of God." The day of wrath and revelation of the righteous judgment of God was the day of judgment that was to be revealed at the destruction of Jerusalem, and the coming in of the gospel kingdom, or the kingdom of God on earth. It was a day of wrath because of the forbearance and long suffering of God toward the Jewish nation, whose sins, like eternal Sinais, had towered to heaven, calling to a sin-avenging God for that awful retribution that not only laid Jerusalem, with all its glory, in the grave, but swallowed up the Jewish empire and swept away its nationality forever. Again, it was a day of wrath against Satan, because it judged him and assigned him his eternal doom.

— "And when ye shall see Jerusalem compassed with armies, then know that the desolation thereof is nigh. Then let them which are in Judea flee to the mountains; and let them which are in the midst of it depart out; and let not them that are in the countries enter thereinto. For these be the days of vengeance, that all things which are written may be fulfilled. But woe unto them that are with child, and to them that give suck in those days! for there shall be great distress in the land, and wrath upon this people."—*Luke*, xxi : 20—23.

The Jews having denied, persecuted and killed the Savior, who came to redeem and save them, their cities, their lands, their economy and their nationality were all given over to desolation and woe, and the glorious kingdom that was promised through the noble line of their holy ancestry, for the salvation of mankind, was now to be ushered in over the death groans of their people, the destruction of their metropolis, and the ruin of their empire, which was truly a day of wrath. While the coming in of the kingdom of the Savior brought liberty and salvation to the Gentiles, it brought vengeance, bondage and wrath to the Jews, and was, therefore, a day of wrath and destruction to them, because of their cruelty and sin against the Son of God.

"For ye, brethren, became followers of the churches of God which in Judea are in Christ Jesus: for ye also have suffered like things of your own countrymen, even as they have of the Jews: Who both killed the Lord Jesus, and their own prophets, and have persecuted us; and they please not God, and are contrary to all men: Forbidding us to speak to the Gentiles that they might be saved, to fill up their sins always: for the wrath is come upon them to the uttermost." —I Thes., ii: 14—16.

This was written but a few years before the awful overthrow of Jerusalem and the destruction of the Jewish nation, and shows that that day was the day of wrath so often alluded to in the Scriptures of Truth, because it was the great day. It was a great day of wrath to the Jews, and a great day of blessing to the Gentiles. It brought destruction and death to the Jews, and salvation and life to the Gentiles. For Christ could not set up his spiritual kingdom on earth until the old, temporal kingdom of the Jewish economy was first destroyed or taken out of the way. Nor will it do to say that the kingdom of Christ was set up on the day of Pentecost, for that was only the baptism of the Holy Ghost, or the shedding forth of the Holy Spirit upon the church at Jerusalem. Christ was not there in his kingdom, nor could he be, until the old kingdom of types and shadows was abolished, the law of rites and ceremonies finished, the temple worship overthrown, the high-priesthood ended, Jerusalem destroyed, and the old covenant taken away, that the new might be established. For the two kingdoms could not exist together upon the earth; the one was to take the place of the other; the Jewish kingdom, with its outward, temporal worship, was to end, and the gospel kingdom, with its inward, spiritual worship, was to begin. And this did not begin at the day of Pentecost. The law of rites and ceremonies, of sacrifice and offering, and the temple worship did not cease on the day of Pentecost, nor for forty years thereafter, or until the great day of His wrath was come upon them to the uttermost; when their city, church and nation were utterly destroyed, and the spiritual kingdom of God established in its place.

"And I beheld when he had opened the sixth seal, and lo, there was a great earthquake; and the sun became black as sackcloth of hair, and the moon became as blood; And the stars of heaven fell unto the earth, even as a fig tree casteth her untimely figs, when she is shaken of a mighty wind. And the heaven departed as a scroll when it is rolled together; and every mountain and island were moved out of their places. And the kings of the earth, and the great men, and the rich men, and the chief captains, and the mighty men, and every bondman, and every freeman, hid themselves in the dens and in the rocks of the mountains, And said to the mountains and rocks, Fall on us, and hide us from the face of him that sitteth on the throne, and from the wrath of the Lamb; For the great day of his wrath is come: and who shall be able to stand?"—*Rev.* vi : 12—17.

This chapter contains one of the seven prophetic histories of the ending of the Jewish religion, and the coming in of the religion of the Savior, as given in the book of Revelation; showing, in all the prophetic grandeur of the Apocalypse, the awe and the glory of that peerless event. The white horse, with his crowned rider going forth conquering and to conquer, was the true symbol of the gospel of Jehovah, brought forth by the blessed Redeemer, first to the Jews and then to the Gentiles. The red horse, with his armed rider that went forth to take peace from the earth, was the terrible symbol of the martial power that was to overthrow and destroy the city and nation of the Jews. The black horse, with his rider holding the balances to measure the wheat and the barley, was the dreadful symbol of the famine to be meted out to the doomed city of Jerusalem; and the pale horse, whose rider was death, was the awful symbol of the destruction and end of the Jewish church and empire, which was soon to be accomplished, when the kingdom of the gospel was to embrace the world. The souls under the altar were the beheaded or slain ones by the Jewish priesthood, whose martyred blood called for the vengeance soon to be poured out, without mixture, upon the Jewish nation. For Christ himself declared, "That upon you may come all the righteous blood shed upon the earth, from the blood of righteous Abel, unto the blood of Zacharias, son of Barachias, whom ye slew between the temple and the altar." —(*Matt.* xxiii : 35.) Although these holy martyrs, who were beheaded or slain for the word of God, had reigned with Christ a thousand years, and enjoyed a season or a dispensation of his glory, yet their blood called for the destruction of the Jewish Church and State, that the word of Gord, for which they were slain, might be established and possess the world.

"And I beheld when he had opened the sixth seal, and lo, there was a great earthquake." This was the breaking up of the Jewish allegiance, and the severing of their nation from the Roman empire.

"And the sun became black as sackcloth of hair." The light of Israel, the Shekina, left the temple, and the glory of God departed from Jerusalem, and the whole nation became enshrouded in their own destruction.

"And the moon became as blood." The Jewish priesthood, together with the temple and its worshippers, fell before the Roman torch and sword. Their priests were slain, their scribes and elders crucified, and their members starved, and mangled in their blood, so that the moon, or Jewish church, became enshrined in blood.

"And the stars of heaven fell unto the earth, even as a fig tree casteth her untimely figs, when she is shaken of a mighty wind." The stars were the righteous and holy followers of Christ and his disciples, who perished in the general slaughter throughout the land of Judea.

"And the heaven departed as a scroll when it is rolled together." "The heaven," the great symbolical economy of the Jews, with all its shadows, types and ceremonies, were rolled up like a scroll and laid away in the archives of eternity, because they were all fulfilled and ended in Christ. -

"And every mountain and island were moved out of their places." These were the rulers, governors and leaders that were continually being raised up, changed, or put down, during the war and siege of Jerusalem.

"And the kings of the earth, and the great men, and the rich men, and the chief captains, and the mighty men, and every bondman, and every freeman, hid themselves in the dens and in the rocks of the mountains." How true was this in reference to the destruction of the Jewish nation; even Josephus himself was concealed in the caverns of the mountains.

"And said to the mountains and rocks, fall on us, and hide us from the face of him that sitteth on the throne." They not only hid themselves beneath the mountains, in the caves of the rocks, and cried for death, but they saw, from the signs and tokens, and the ruin around them, that their destruction was from God. They now saw, when it was too late, that the blood of the murdered prophets, the crucified Savior and the martyred saints was working a fearful retribution before the face of him that sitteth on the throne. That their city, their church and their empire were ending, and that a new kingdom, throne and dominion were being established in its stead, which was the glorious kingdom of the gospel of Chirst.

"And from the wrath of the Lamb." This was the Lamb of God who once wept over Jerusalem, and would have gathered her children as a hen gathereth her brood under her wings, but they would not hearken to his voice, nor believe the teachings of his love, but persecuted, condemned and killed him, and despised and slew his followers until they saw the heavens bending with his glory, and their nation writhing and dying beneath the hand of his power and the ire of his law.

"For the great day of his wrath is come; and who shall be able to stand?" This was truly a great day. It was not only a day of stupendous and awful issues, but it was a day of wrath upon the enemies of Christ. Events, great and mighty, were transpiring. The law of sacrifice and offerings was closing, the types and shadows were ending, the temple worship was ceasing, the Jewish church was expiring, the great city was burning, the Hebrew nation was dying, and the promises of Jehovah were fulfilling. The kingdom of Christ was descending, the curse of original sin was ending, the graves of trespasses and sins were opening, the kingdom of Satan was trembling, and the judgment was established. It was truly the great day of God's wrath against Satan, the great Prince of Sin and Death, as well as against the wicked and rebellious Jews. And it is still the great day of judgment against all who do wickedly; every evil thought, word and action is condemned by the Judge, and every good thought, word and action is approved by him. This every candid heart must confess; for our hearts will either approve or condemn us for our words and actions, and God is greater than our hearts, and will also approve or condemn us. Well may it be asked: "Who shall be able to stand?" But, thanks be to God, though we sin, we have an Advocate in our Judge, who can be touched with the feeling of our infirmities, and who, if we confess our sins, is faithful and just to forgive us our sins, and who will not only make us able to stand, but will give us, at death and the final judgment, a crown of life in everlasting joy.

"But the Lord shall endure forever: he hath prepared his throne for judgment. And he shall judge the world in righteousness, he shall minister judgment to the people in uprightness."—*Psa.* ix: 7—8.

The great spiritual throne of God's judgment was prepared in heaven, and at the proper time, when all things were fulfilled, the blessed Redeemer, the Supreme Judge of the world, descended upon his throne to judge the world in righteousness, and to "minister judgment to the people in uprightness;" which shows that the world is now before the Judge, and that He is ministering judgment to the people in this, the gospel or judgment day.

"Many seek the ruler's favor; but every man's judgment cometh from the Lord."—*Prov.* xxix: 26.

This not only shows us that judgment is upon the children of men, but that no man can avoid it, however much they may court the ruler's favor, or seek relief among the powers of earth; "for every man's judgment cometh from the Lord," and not from man, so that all men are now being judged by the Lord.

"Thou didst cause judgment to be heard from heaven; the earth feared and was still."—*Psa.*, lxxvi: 8.

Judgment has already been heard from heaven, and this shows us plainly that mankind have not to wait until the end of the world for it, but that it has long been on earth, and is still going on. For the Lord "didst cause judgment to be heard from heaven; the earth feared and was still."

"A bruised reed shall he not break, and smoking flax shall he not quench, till he send forth judgment unto victory."—*Matt.*, xii: 20.

A bruised reed is an emblem of weak and feeble persons, crushed with difficulties, whom Christ declared should not be broken. The smoking fllax, or the wick of the ancient lamps that was almost extinguished, should not be quenched. He will bring forth judgment to victory; He will raise up the feeble, and, by His judgment, make them stronger than their foes. He will not quench the smoking flax, or the poor, benighted, helpless souls, but will light them into a sacred flame of love, and send forth judgment unto victory for them, until Satan and all his dark hosts shall be overthrown before them. O, it is glorious for the Christian to know that the blessed

Redeemer is ever, by his judgment, giving him victory over all his foes.

"For God shall bring every work into judgment, with every secret thing, whether it be good, or whether it be evil."—*Eccl.*, xii : 14.

Every thought, word and action that we shall think, speak or do, whether it be good, or whether it be evil, shall be immediately brought into judgment. This is the reason why we are immediately condemned in our heart or conscience when we do a bad action; it is the judgment of God that condemns us. And this is the reason why we feel happy when we do a good action; it is the judgment of God that justifies us, and shows us that the judgment is now going on, and that immediately after death, the righteous Judge will fix our state forever, according to our actions in life. O, may the Lord help us to live the life of the righteous, that we may die the death of the godly and meet a righteous reward at the judgment seat of Christ.

"But why dost thou judge thy brother? or why dost thou set at nought thy brother? for we shall all stand before the judgment-seat of Christ."—*Rom.*, xiv : 10.

The judgment-seat of Christ is ✿ in the spirit world, and his judgment embraces this world and extends to every son and daughter of man; and as the gospel kingdom is a spiritual kingdom, so is the judgment a spiritual judgment, and all are under the judgment while they are in the world, and as soon as the natural body is dead, the spiritual body stands before the judgment seat of Christ, where it hears the verdict or judgment of the Judge that decides its destiny. For it is appointed unto men once to die, but after this the judgment. O, may we all be prepared to stand before the judgment seat of Christ!

"We are confident, I say, and willing rather to be absent from the body, and to be present with the Lord. Wherefore we labor, that, whether present or absent, we may be accepted of him. For we must all appear before the judgment-seat of Christ; that every one may receive the things done in his body, according to that he hath done, whether it be good or bad."—II *Cor.*, v : 8—10.

To be absent from the body is to be separated from the natural body by death. Indeed, we cannot be present with Christ until we drop this body of flesh and blood, and appear in the spiritual body before the judgment-seat of Christ, that every one may receive his reward for the things done in his body, whether they be good or bad. Hence, it is evident that we are judged here for every thought, word and action, as we are borne along the journey of life and time; that as soon as we die we may receive the decision of the Judge according to the judgment wherewith he hath judged us, in accordance with our actions, whether they be good or bad. Again; observe that the apostle says: "And willing rather to be absent from the body, and to be present with the Lord," and "that every one may receive *the things* DONE IN THE BODY," thus showing that to be present with God, we must leave the body behind; and as the general belief, that the judgment is not to occur until time shall end, is founded upon the idea that the body must be judged, which, of course, could not occur without its resurrection, and as it is evident from this passage that the body is not to be raised, it is, therefore, also clear that the judgment is immediate. Further; it is not the body that is to "receive," but *the man* is to "receive the things *done in the body;*" that is, the body has no part in the rewards and punishments—is not judged.

"And he commanded us to preach unto the people, and to testify that it is he which was ordained of God to be the Judge of quick and dead."—*Acts*, x: 42.

By this, we are told that our blessed Savior was ordained of God to be the Judge of both the living and the dead, for the quick are the living; so that it is plain that mankind are judged while they are living for their actions in life, and receive the final sentence or judgment as soon as the natural body is dead, that assigns the soul or spiritual body, which is the real man, to weal or woe, according to its life on earth. Otherwise, Christ could not be the Judge of the living and the dead.

(* * * * "For when the Gentiles, which have not the law, do by nature the things contained in the law, these having not the law, are a law unto themselves : Which show the work of the law written in their hearts, their conscience also bearing witness, and their thoughts the meanwhile accusing, or else excusing one another:) In the day when God shall judge the secrets of men by Jesus Christ, according to my gospel."—*Rom.* ii : 14—16.

This shows the love and goodness of our blessed Redeemer in giving all the children of men the advantage of his gospel and judgment; whether they have the written word or not, they all now, since the coming of Christ in his gospel kingdom, have a law unto themselves which is "The true Light, which lighteth every man that cometh into the world."—(*John*, i : 9.) For, being resurrected out of the graves of trespass and sin, from under the curse of original transgression, Christ has shown the work of the law written in their hearts, their consciences bearing witness before God, the Judge of all the earth; their thoughts, meanwhile, accusing or else excusing one another, so that they are now without excuse, and have been since the gospel day has been established on earth. For the day here spoken of was the gospel day, when God should judge the secrets of men by Jesus Christ, according to the gospel, but was not yet established when the apostle wrote this epistle, nor for some years afterward.

" And if any man hear my words, and believe not, I judge him not : for I come not to judge the world, but to save the world. He that rejecteth me, and receiveth not my words, hath one that judgeth him : the word that I have spoken, the same shall judge him in the last day."—*John*, xii : 47—48.

Christ did not come to judge the world at his first coming ; He came, as the Savior, to save the world. It was at his second coming, when he set up his gospel kingdom, that he came to judge the world by his gospel, which day is the gospel day, and is the last day of man's probation on earth. There is no other day after this, the gospel day, that man can repent and be saved, so that the gospel day is the judgment day, or the last day ; and as it is the word of Christ, or the gospel, that judgeth, it is evident that the gospel day is the judgment day, because it is the last day of man's probation or trial.

" And this is the Father's will which hath sent me, that of all which he hath given me I should lose nothing, but should raise it up again at the last day. And this is the will of him that sent me, that every one which seeth the Son, and believeth on him, may have everlasting life : and I will raise him up at the last day."—*John*, vi : 39—40.

As the Father gave the Son the whole human race as his purchase, and as he was the second Adam, to raise up all that the first Adam had cast down, it is evident that he lost nothing of what the Father had given him ; for he raised all mankind up out of the graves of trespass and sin, from under the curse of the law, at the last day, which is the gospel day, and placed them all within the pale of redemption, where all who will come, may come and be saved. For it is the will of the Father that every one which seeth the Son, and believeth on him, should have everlasting life, and that Christ should, by his holy word, raise them up at the last day, or the gospel day, which is the judgment day into glory.

" In those days, and at that time, will I cause the Branch of right-eousness to grow up unto David; and he shall execute judgment and righteousness in the land."—*Jer.* xxxiii : 15.

This shows us that Christ, who is the righteous Branch, as soon as he possessed the throne of David, or was come in his spiritual kingdom, was to execute judgment and righteous-ness in the land; that it was not deferred until the end of time, but, in words as plain as human language can teach, we are taught that at that time he will cause the Branch of right-cousness to grow up unto David; and he shall execute judg-ment and righteousness in the land; which is now everywhere going on.

" Judge me, O Lord my God, according to thy righteousness; and let them not rejoice over me."—*Psa.*, xxxv : 24.

The king of Israel knew that the Lord was judging in the earth, or he would not have asked him to judge him according to his righteousness, that his enemies might not rejoice over him, and thus shows to all that the judgment is in the earth.

" I will judge thee in the place where thou wast created, in the land of thy nativity."—*Eze.*, xxi : 30.

This shows us plainly that the judgment is going on in the earth, or the Lord would not have said : "I will judge thee in the place where thou wast created, in the land of thy na-tivity." Hence, all are judged in this world, and in the place where they have their existence.

" For thou hast maintained my right and my cause ; thou satest in the throne judging right."—*Psa.*, ix : 4.

By this, we understand that the Lord is not only seated in the throne of judgment, but that he is judging the children of men ; not going to judge at the end of the world, but that he is now in the throne judging right.

" Say among the heathen that the Lord reigneth ; the world also shall be established that it shall not be moved: he shall judge the people righteously. Let the heavens rejoice, and let the earth be glad ; let the sea roar, and the fulness thereof. Let the field be joy-ful, and all that is therein ; then shall all the trees of the wood rejoice before the Lord ; for he cometh, for he cometh to judge the earth : he shall judge the world with righteousness, and the people with his truth."—*Psa.*, xcvi : 10—13.*

This is a beautiful description of the coming and reign of our blessed Savior in his spiritual or gospel kingdom on earth.

---

*Verse 10 is commented on on page 23.

It was to be said or preached among the heathen or Gentiles, "that the Lord reigneth;" that Christ was on the throne of his spiritual dominion; that the world was to be established —not burned up or destroyed; that it should not even be moved—and that He should judge the people righteously. Human language could not give a clearer description of the gospel or judgment day than this; especially when the heavens were told to rejoice, the earth to be glad, the sea to roar, the field to be joyful, and the trees of the wood to "rejoice before the Lord; for he cometh to judge the earth: he shall judge the world with righteousness, and the people with his truth." That this is Christ's second coming is evident from the fact that he came to judge the world; his first coming was to redeem the world and not to judge it; and as the gospel of that redemption was to be preached in all the world for a witness to the nations, before the end of the old natural Jewish religion and the beginning of the new spiritual religion of Christ, it is everywhere plain that this is the period alluded to. As Christ's second coming was entirely a spiritual coming, none but spiritual eyes could behold him. His first coming was in the flesh, but his second coming was in the spirit, and none but spiritual beings accompanied him. The cherubic numbers, the angel hosts and the sainted millions of the redeemed, composed the retinue of his descending kingdom. The song of triumph, the harps of glory, the immortal nations and the splendors of Immanuel were all unheard and unseen by mortals. But the breaking up of the Hebrew empire, the ending of their religion, the slaughtering of their nation, the falling of their dynasty, the burning of their city, the passing away of their dispensation, the fulfilment of the promises of God and the coming in of a new era astonished the nations, and the listening world felt that something more than mortal was transpiring on earth. Yet the faithful followers of the Savior understood the meaning of those mighty events; they knew that as soon as the law of rites and ceremonies was abolished, the types and shadows done away, the temple worship overthrown, Jerusalem destroyed, and the Jewish nationality ended, the Son of God would come, according to his promise, in his kingdom, dethrone Satan and set up his gospel kingdom and establish his throne of judgment and pardon on earth, where all the sons and daughters of our race can find salvation, happiness and eternal life. This is the reason why the king of

Israel cried out, more than a thousand years before the coming of Christ in his spiritual kingdom, "Let the heavens rejoice, let the earth be glad, let the field be joyful, and let all the trees of the wood rejoice before the Lord, for he cometh to judge the earth : he shall judge the world with righteousness, and the people with his truth." For, in the judgment, the world is to be established and the people judged righteously, which shows that the judgment day is the gospel day.

" And in mercy shall the throne be established: and he shall sit upon it in truth in the tabernacle of David, judging, and seeking judgment, and hasting righteousness."—*Isa.*, xvi: 5.

Our blessed Savior, according to the flesh, was a descendant of the tabernacle or house of David, and as David sat upon the earthly throne of the earthly Israel, so does Christ sit upon the spiritual throne of the spiritual Israel, "judging, and seeking judgment, and hasting righteousness." For the moment the earthly kingdom and economy of the house of David was ended, that moment Christ ascended the spiritual throne and set up his spiritual or gospel kingdom on earth, where he is "judging and seeking judgment, and hasting righteousness" by the gospel of salvation.

" The Lord executeth righteousness and judgment for all that are oppressed."—*Psa.*, ciii: 6.

The Lord executeth righteousness and judgment all the time; He does not wait until the end of the world, but he executeth it now, for this is in the present tense, which shows to all that the judgment is now going on in the gospel kingdom.

" And as he reasoned of righteousness, temperance, and judgment to come, Felix trembled, and answered, Go thy way for this time ; when I have a convenient season, I will call for thee."—*Acts*, xxiv : 25.

As Christ had not yet come in his spiritual or gospel kingdom to establish the throne of his judgment, the apostle could not reason any other way than of the judgment to come. For he knew that as soon as the old covenant of carnal commandments was taken away, the new would be established, and that Christ would come in his spiritual kingdom to execute judgment and righteousness in the earth.

" The men of Nineveh shall rise in the judgment with this generation, and shall condemn it : because they repented at the preaching of Jonas ; and behold, a greater than Jonas is here."—*Matt.*, xii : 41.

The great object of Christ was to show the dreadful wickedness of the Jews in rejecting him as the Savior of the world.

They had the promises of God which they saw fulfilled in him; they had their law that pointed him out as the Messiah; they had the types and shadows that all along prefigured him; they had the prophets that everywhere told of him; they had his godly and holy life that showed him more than mortal; they had his miracles that proved him the promised Savior; they saw his power and beheld his glory, and yet they persecuted, scourged and killed him, so that the wicked inhabitants of Nineveh, in comparison with them, in the gospel or judgment day, will condemn them, for they repented at the preaching of Jonas and turned to God; but the Jews would not repent, even at the preaching of the Messiah himself. Hence, the men of Nineveh shall rise, in the gospel day or judgment
● day, far above the men of Judea in comparative virtue and goodness before God and man. And, O, how should we, of this day, take this lesson home to our own hearts, and ask ourselves how much better we are than the Jews! We have the same law and the prophets they had; we have all the promises, signs and warnings they had; we have heard the same teachings, works and miracles of Christ they saw and heard; we have heard the preachings and instructions of the apostles as they did, and we have the lives of the martyrs, and the power and influence of the church, which they had not; and more than this, we have the dreadful example God made of them for their wickedness, and yet many of us have not repented and turned to Christ. O, may God help us to repent and come to him, that we may not be condemned in the judgment.

"The queen of the south shall rise up in the judgment with the men of this generation, and condemn them: for she came from the utmost parts of the earth, to hear the wisdom of Solomon; and behold, a greater than Solomon is here."—*Luke*, xi: 31.

The queen of the south was a heathen queen, over a heathen nation, and she heard of the wisdom and holy religion of Solomon, king of Israel, and resolving to know the truth for herself, she, without any invitation, or even knowing whether she would be received by that great man, started on her long journey and finally reached the palace of Solomon, where she found that the half had not been told. But the wicked Jews, after hearing and seeing the wisdom, power and glory of Jesus Christ, which was transcendently greater than that of Solomon, would not even believe the Son of God, but cast him out and put him to death; so that the queen of the south, in this gospel or judgment day, rises far above the Jews in the judgment, and shows to all the world the dreadful ingratitude and wickedness of the Jews in rejecting the blessed Redeemer; "for she came from the utmost parts of the earth to hear the wisdom of Solomon; and behold, a greater than Solomon is here."

"But into whatsoever city ye enter, and they receive you not, go your ways out into the streets of the same, and say, Even the very dust of your city which cleaveth on us, we do wipe off against you: notwithstanding, be ye sure of this, that the kingdom of God is come nigh unto you. But I say unto you, That it shall be more tolerable in that day for Sodom than for that city. Woe unto thee, Chorazin! woe unto thee, Bethsaida! for if the mighty works had been done in Tyre and Sidon, which have been done in you, they had a great while ago repented, sitting in sackcloth and ashes. But it shall be more tolerable for Tyre and Sidon at the judgment, than for you."—*Luke*, x: 10–14.

When the Savior sent out his disciples to preach the gospel, he gave them power to heal the sick, cast out devils, and work miracles; that they might everywhere prove to the world the truth of his mission, and to tell the people that the kingdom of God, or the gospel kingdom, was nigh unto them, and that if they would not now receive the gospel, under all these evidences, that it would be more tolerable in that day, that is, the day of the kingdom of God, the gospel or judgment day, for Sodom than for that city or people, "Woe unto thee, Chorazin! Woe unto thee, Bethsaida! for if the mighty works," the healing of the sick, the casting out of devils, and the raising of the dead, "had been done in Tyre and Sidon, which have been done in you, they had a great while ago repented in sackcloth and ashes. But it shall be more tolerable for Tyre and Sidon at the judgment than for you." As the kingdom of God that was then nigh at hand, and shortly after did come and destroy Jerusalem and those wicked Jews, together with their religion, and brought in the spiritual reign of Christ and his judgment; and as Tyre and Sidon, of the heathen, and Chorazin and Bethsaida, of the Jews, were given us as examples of the judgments of God for their wickedness, we can now see in this, the gospel day, or judgment day, that it is indeed more tolerable for Tyre and Sidon, who knew not God, than for Chorazin and Bethsaida, who knew God, but continued in sin and wickedness until they were destroyed. And O, may we all take warning by the awful example.

"For if we sin wilfully after we have received the knowledge of the truth, there remaineth no more sacrifice for sins, But a certain fearful looking for of judgment and fiery indignation, which shall devour the adversaries."—*Heb.*, x: 26—27.

If we wilfully turn away from Christ, after having embraced his holy doctrine, and reject his gospel after having known its efficacy, and refuse to trust the Savior for salvation, then "there remaineth no more sacrifice tor sin, But a certain fearful looking for of judgment and fiery indignation" that devour the adversaries of God. This is the judgment that takes place immediately after death, where and when every apostate, and all who die wicked, are judged and sent to the world of fiery indignation and torment forever. O, may God help us to hold fast to the gospel of Christ unto the end, that we may all receive from our righteous Judge a crown of life.

● "The Lord knoweth how to deliver the godly out of temptation, and to reserve the unjust unto the day of judgment to be punished.— II. *Peter*, ii: 9.

The unjust are those who, by cheating, fraud and oppression, grow rich and enjoy the world and its pleasures. They are reserved unto the day of their death, which is the day of judgment, ("for it is appointed unto men once to die, but after this the judgment") for their punishment. The unjust are like the swine, merely fattening for destruction. They are reserved unto the day of judgment to be punished, or rather their punishment then begins. For as soon as the natural body is dead, the spirit appears at the judgment seat of Christ and receives its final reward; so that this Scripture, like the preceding one, has a direct reference to the judgment after death.

"Of the doctrine of baptisms, and of laying on of hands, and of resurrection of the dead, and of eternal judgment."—*Heb.*, vi: 2.

The judgment, in this passage, being coupled with doctrines and ordinances that are continually going on, shows that the judgment is not only eternal in its decisions and consequences, but that it is eternally going on also, and that mankind are everywhere being judged and tried as they pass along in life and time, and receive the final verdict after death, that assigns to heaven or hell, according to the deeds done in the body.

"Let the heavens be glad, and let the earth rejoice: and let men say among the nations, The Lord reigneth. Let the sea roar, and the fullness thereof: let the fields rejoice, and all that is therein. Then shall the trees of the wood sing out at the presence of the Lord, because he cometh to judge the earth."—I. *Chron.*, xvi: 31—33.

This is a beautiful promise of the coming of Christ's kingdom and his spiritual reign on earth. The heavens were to be glad, and the earth was to rejoice, (and not be burned up as some would have it,) and men were to say among the nations, "The Lord reigneth. This is the reign of our blessed Lord in his gospel kingdom." "Then shall the trees of the wood sing out at the presence of the Lord, because he cometh to judge the earth." This was the glorious coming in of the gospel day, when Christ came and set up the throne of his judgment in the earth.

" O Lord, thou hast seen my wrong: judge thou my cause."—*Lam.* iii : 59.

This Scripture teaches us that the judgment was going on in earth at the time of its utterance; for if there was then no judgment, the holy prophet would not have asked the Lord to judge his cause.

" And I saw heaven opened, and behold, a white horse; and he that sat upon him was called Faithful and True, and in righteousness he doth judge and make war."—*Rev.*, xix: 11.

"And I saw heaven opened." This was the preparation for the coming gospel. "And behold a white horse." This was the throne and kingdom of the gospel in its victorious grandeur. "And he that sat upon him was called Faithful and True." This is the great King of the gospel kingdom, whose spiritual dominion is over all the earth. " And in righteousness doth he judge and make war." This not only shows us that the gospel kingdom or gospel day is the day of judgment, but it shows that in righteousness doth he judge; not that he is going to judge at the end of time, but that he *doth* judge and make war here and now on earth among men; so that the judgment day is the gospel day.

"So that we ourselves glory in you in the churches of God, for your patience and faith in all your persecutions and tribulations that ye endure : Which is a manifest token of the righteous judgment of God, that ye may be counted worthy of the kingdom of God, for which ye also suffer."—II. *Thes.*, i: 4—5.

The apostles were all glorying in the faithful membership of the churches of God, for their patience and faith, under the persecutions and tribulations they endured while waiting for the promised kingdom; which endurance was not only a manifest token of the righteous judgment of God being near at hand, but that they were accounted worthy of the kingdom of God for which they suffered, when it should come. For this kingdom was to bring judgment, righteousness and eternal happiness to every faithful believer in Christ.

" And dost thou open thine eyes upon such a one, and bringest me into judgment with thee?"—*Job*, xiv: 3.

This, also, shows us that men are brought into judgment with the Lord while here on earth, for Job was alive and on the earth when he was thus brought into judgment.

" Harken unto me, my people; and give ear unto me, O my nation: for a law shall proceed from me, and I will make my judgment to rest for a light of the people."—*Isa.*, li: 4.

This is another glorious promise in the prophecy of God, of the coming of the gospel kingdom. The Redeemer calls unto his people and nation to give ear; that a law, which is the gospel law, (for they had the old law already,) shall proceed from him, and that he would make his judgment to rest for a light to the people; which clearly shows that the gospel and the judgment came together, and that mankind are now under the light of both the gospel and the judgment.

" I can of mine own self do nothing: as I hear, I judge: and my judgment is just: because I seek not mine own will, but the will of the Father which hath sent me."—*John*, v: 30.

No plainer evidence of a present judgment can be given in the language of man than that of the above Scripture. Our blessed Savior says: "As I hear, I judge;" that is, as the actions of men come to pass, they are judged by him; and his judgment is just, because he seeks not his own will but the will of the Father which sent him. He does not wait until the end of time to judge the children of men, but as he hears, or as the deeds of men transpire, he judges them; so that mankind are now everywhere being judged in the gospel day.

" And the angels which kept not their first estate, but left their own habitation, he hath reserved in everlasting chains under darkness unto the judgment of the great day."—*Jude*, vi.

These were beings of another world or principality, who kept not their first estate, but left their own habitation and fell into sin and became devils, under a great chief called the devil, whilst they are called his angels. These were the angels that God charged with folly, (as in *Job*, iv: 18,) and the devil is the chief whom Christ beheld as lightning fall from heaven (*Luke*, x: 18); and these are the angels that God spared not, but cast them down to hell and delivered them in chains of darkness to be reserved unto judgment (II. *Peter*, ii: 4), which agrees with what is said above: that God hath reserved them in everlasting chains under darkness unto the judgment of the great day. Their being chained does not mean that they are literally chained and handcuffed in their prison of woe, but that that they are held in on all sides by the power of God, with no hope or prospect of escape forever. Thus limited in their work of malevolence and ruin, the devil and his angels have no power over the children of men, more than that of temptation. Before the coming of Christ at the great day, when he set up his spiritual kingdom on earth, the Devil, or Satan, held all mankind in the graves of trespass and sins into which he had lured them by temptation, and by which he ruled the world and triumphed over man, until the coming in of the gospel kingdom of Christ, when mankind were resurrected from the graves of sin and death. For "now is the judgment of this world: now shall the prince of this world be cast out."—(*John*, xii: 31.) This is the judgment of the great day. The blessed Savior came and cast out the prince of this world, which is the Devil and Satan, established his gospel kingdom and resurrected the sons and daughters of men into all its rights and privileges, where, by calling on Christ, the weakest child of man can conquer Satan, triumph over death and rise to immortality and eternal life. Thus is the prince of this world, which is Satan, judged and conquered by Christ, so that his power on earth shall thenceforward decline until he shall be utterly subdued, and sin and death destroyed and the earth restored to its primitive glory. Hence, the gospel day is the day of judgment, because the prince of this world is judged (*John*, xvi: 11), and his kingdom is being destroyed by the power of the gospel of Christ.

" Of the increase of his government and peace there shall be no end, upon the throne of David, and upon his kingdom, to order it, and to establish it with judgment and with justice from henceforth even forever. The zeal of the Lord of hosts will perform this."—*Isa.*, ix : 7.

The government, to the increase of which there shall be no end, is the peaceful government of the gospel of the Redeemer, which was established at the end of the Jewish economy and shall go on increasing forever; while the kingdom of Satan shall decrease until it is entirely destroyed and the world brought back to its Eden grandeur. The throne and kingdom of David, that was to be established with judgment and justice from thenceforth and forever, is the throne and gospel kingdom of the Savior, set up at the overthrow of Jerusalem, so that the gospel and the judgment were both established at the same time, and are now both going on among men.

" For the Son of man shall come in the glory of his Father, with his angels; and then he shall reward every man according to his works. Verily I say unto you, There be some standing here, which shall not taste of death, till they see the Son of man coming in his kingdom."—*Matt.*, xvi : 27—28.

As the Son of Man had already come once, this, of course, was to be his second coming, and as there were some then standing there, who were not to die until they saw him come the second time, it is evident that that coming was near at hand; and as he was to come in the glory of his Father with his angels, it is plain that it was a spiritual coming; and as he was to reward every man according to his works when he did come, and as that could not be done without judging them, it must be clear to all that his second coming was the coming in of the gospel kingdom, in which salvation and the judgment were established on earth.

" So likewise ye, when ye see these things come to pass, know ye that the kingdom of God is nigh at hand. Verily, I say unto you, this generation shall not pass away till all be fulfilled."—*Luke*, xxi : 31—32.

The things that were to come to pass before the coming of the kingdom of God, were the signs that presaged the destruction of Jerusalem, and when they saw these things, then they were to know that the kingdom of God was nigh at hand, which shows that the destruction of Jerusalem and the coming of the gospel kingdom were parts of the same great event. And that generation not passing away until Jerusalem was destroyed, and the kingdom of the gospel of God established, shows how near at hand the second coming of Christ then was, for as Christ had already come in the flesh, this, of course, was to be his second coming, and that in the spirit; for his gospel kingdom is spiritual, having a spiritual religion, a spiritual judgment, and a spiritual salvation.

" Which also said, Ye men of Galilee, why stand ye gazing up into heaven? this same Jesus which is taken up from you into heaven, shall so come in like manner as ye have seen him go into heaven."—*Acts*, i: 11.

It was the spiritual body of our blessed Lord, filled with all the fulness of the Godhead, that ascended to heaven, so that none but spiritual eyes could behold him, and no eyes but those of his disciples did behold his ascension from earth, and had they not been in spiritual communication with him, they could not have seen him ascending to glory. So, in like manner, when he descended in his kingdom, none but spiritual eyes could behold him. For "this same Jesus which is taken up from you into heaven, shall so come in like manner as ye have seen him go into heaven." Therefore, being spiritual, both in Being and kingdom, he can only be spiritually discerned, so that none but those who were in actual spiritual communication with the blessed Redeemer, could see him, either ascending or descending. For none can see God and live. Hence, it is plain that the gospel kingdom is a spiritual kingdom, and that the judgment is a spiritual judgment, and that God is a spirit and must be worshiped in spirit and in truth.

" And when he was demanded of the Pharisees, when the kingdom of God should come, he answered them and said, The kingdom of God cometh not with observation."—*Luke*, xvii : 20.

In this Christ plainly told the Pharisees that " the kingdom of God cometh not with observation." That is, it would come without being observed by the children of men on earth, because the kingdom of the gospel is of a spiritual character, and cannot be seen by natural eyes. It can only be seen by those who are in spiritual communion with Christ. It, therefore, came without observation, or without being observed by men of earth, and is now controlling the energies and shaping the destiny of the world.

" Whosoever therefore shall be ashamed of me, and my words, in this adulterous and sinful generation; of him also shall the Son of man be ashamed, when he cometh in the glory of his Father with the holy angels. And he said unto them, Verily, I say unto you, That there be some of them that stand here which shall not taste of death, till they have seen the kingdom of God come with power."— *Mark*, viii : 38, *and* ix : 1.

In this Scripture, the Savior not only tells us that he would come again, but that those who were now ashamed of him, he would be ashamed of when he came in the glory of his Father with the holy angels, and that there were some standing there then, who would not die until they had seen the kingdom of God come with power. These were some of the holy followers of Christ, who were in spiritual communion with the Son of God, and would live to see Jerusalem destroyed, and the kingdom come with power and be established on earth for the glory of God and the salvation of man.

" And this gospel of the kingdom shall be preached in all the world, for a witness unto all nations; and then shall the end come. When ye, therefore, shall see the abomination of desolation, spoken of by Daniel the prophet, stand in the holy place, (whoso readeth, let him understand,) Then let them which be in Judea flee into the mountains."—*Matt.*, xxiv : 14—16.

The gospel of the kingdom was to be preached in all the world; that is, in all the then known world, for a witness unto all nations, which was done before the second coming of Christ at the destruction of Jerusalem, and then the end was to come —the end of the Jewish church and its economy; the end of the Hebrew dispensation and nationality; and the beginning of the gospel reign of our Lord Jesus Christ. The abomi-nation of desolation, spoken of by Daniel, the prophet, standing in the holy place, was the eagles of the Roman standards, regarded as objects of idolatrous worship, set up around Jerusalem and, afterward, in the temple. Whoso readeth, let him understand that the destruction foretold by the prophet Daniel, more than five hundred years before, was now being fulfilled. Fleeing into the mountains was to save themselves, that is, the Christians, and prevent their being taken by the Romans. (See the New Testament, with notes, as published by the American Tract Society.)

"For as the lightning cometh out of the east, and shineth even unto the west; so shall also the coming of the Son of man be. For wheresoever the carcass is, there will the eagles be gathered together."—*Matt.*, xxiv : 27—28.

This shows that the second coming of the Son of Man was to be a spiritual coming; like the lightning, quick and powerful, and can never be seen only in its revelation. "Wheresoever the carcass is, there will the eagles be." Wherever the Jews are, or the dying Jewish nation is, the Romans will be upon them, as eagles are upon their prey—the eagle being the ordinary standard of the Roman armies; which shows, beyond all contradiction, that Christ did come the second time at the destruction of Jerusalem, in his lightning or spiritual kingdom, and established the throne of his gospel judgment on the earth.

"Two women shall be grinding at the mill; the one shall be taken, and the other left. Watch therefore; for ye know not what hour your Lord doth come."—*Matt.*, xxiv : 41—42.

By this Scripture all can see that the second coming of Christ was at the destruction of Jerusalem, where the women did the grinding on mills prepared for that purpose, two to each mill. One was taken as a follower of Christ, and saved, while the other was left to perish through unbelief and rejection of him. And the disciples were then and there commanded to watch, for they knew not what hour the Lord would come, but that his second coming would be in the day when two women would be grinding at the mill, which was the custom when Jerusalem was destroyed.

"So that ye come behind in no gift; waiting for the coming of our Lord Jesus Christ."—I. *Cor.*, 1 : 7.

The members of the church at Corinth were admonished to see that they came behind in no spiritual gift, while they were waiting for the second coming of Christ, and the admonition was written only about thirteen years before he was to appear in the gospel kingdom, when he would end the Hebrew kingdom and economy, set up his own glorious gospel kingdom, and begin his spiritual reign of redemption and judgment on earth.

" To the end he may establish your hearts unblamable in holiness before God, even our Father, at the coming of our Lord Jesus Christ with all his saints."—I. *Thes.*, iii : 13.

This was spoken but a few years before the second coming of Christ, at the end of the Jewish dispensation, and shows that these Thessalonian brethren were to live until Christ did come in his spiritual kingdom, or he would not have told them to have their hearts established unblamable before God, at the coming of the Lord Jesus Christ with all his saints. And as they did live until the Jewish kingdom was ended, and the old covenant taken out of the way, it is evident that they lived until the new was established, for that was to be done as soon as the old was taken away.

" And the very God of peace sanctify you wholly ; and I pray God your whole spirit, and soul, and body, be preserved blameless unto the coming of our Lord Jesus Christ."—I. *Thes.*, v : 23.

This is so plain that every reader must see that the second coming of Christ was at the end of the Jewish age, or the destruction of Jerusalem, as the Thessalonian brethren were to be preserved, soul and body, blameless unto the coming of the Lord Jesus Christ ; that is, they were to live righteously in the body until Christ came and set up his gospel kingdom on earth, under the reign of which all mankind are now living, and are being judged according to their actions in life.

" Be patient therefore, brethren, unto the coming of the Lord. Behold, the husbandman waiteth for the precious fruit of the earth, and hath long patience for it, until he receive the early and latter rain.—Be ye also patient; establish your hearts : for the coming of the Lord draweth nigh."—*James* v : 7—8.

As this was written to the people of Israel only about twelve years before the second advent of Christ, when he established the throne of his spiritual or gospel kingdom in the earth, it might well be said that "The coming of the Lord draweth nigh," and that they should be patient unto the coming of the Lord. Hence, the promise of his coming was always made to that generation in which he did come, and proves beyond all doubt that the apostle not only entreated the Christians of the twelve tribes to wait patiently for the coming of the Lord Jesus, but that the time was drawing nigh when he would appear and set up his spiritual kingdom, plant the economy of his gospel, and establish the throne of his judgment in the earth.

"And now, little children, abide in him; that when he shall appear, we may have confidence, and not be ashamed before him at his coming."—I, *John*, ii : 28.

This Scripture teaches us, that those little children, or true believers, were to abide in Christ, that when he appeared in his kingdom they might have confidence, and not be ashamed before him at his coming, which shows us plainly that they were to live until Christ's second coming, when he would establish his kingdom on the earth.

"That thou keep this commandment without spot, unrebukable until the appearing of our Lord Jesus Christ."—I. *Tim.*, vi : 14.

By this, we are taught that Christ was to appear the second time while Timothy still lived; for the inspired apostle tells him to keep this commandment without spot, unrebukable, until the appearing of our Lord Jesus Christ. And as our blessed Lord had appeared the first time, suffered and died and ascended to glory, this, of course, was to be his second appearing; and as Timothy himself was told to keep the commandment until the appearing of our Lord Jesus Christ, it is evident that he was to live until Christ did come, which was only about seven years after this was written to him ; so that it is as plain as human language can make it, that Timothy was to live until the Son of God came again, the second time, and established the kingdom of his gospel and the throne of his judgment in the earth; that whosoever would come, might come and be saved.

"Looking for that blessed hope, and the glorious appearing of the great God, and our Savior Jesus Christ."—*Titus*, ii : 13.

As all the Scriptures on the second coming of Christ affirm that he would appear before the consummation of the then existing generation, it was natural that the Christians of that day should look for the fulfilment of that blessed hope. They had everywhere heard in the promises of Christ concerning his coming kingdom, that they should look for it as being immediate, while they lived on earth. This is the reason why the great apostle wrote to Titus to live "godly in this present world, Looking for that blessed hope and the glorious appearing of the great God, and our Savior Jesus Christ." And as Titus was to look for the glorious appearing of Christ while he lived in this present world, it is evident that the coming throne and kingdom of Christ was near at hand when the apostle wrote his letter to Titus, for it was only about seven years after that Christ did come and set up the kingdom of his gospel and the throne of his judgment in the earth.

" But the day of the Lord will come as a thief in the night ; in the which the heavens shall pass away with a great noise, and the elements shall melt with fervent heat, the earth also and the works that are therein shall be burned up. Seeing then that all these things shall be dissolved, what manner of persons ought ye to be in all holy conversation and godliness, Looking for and hasting unto the coming of the day of God, wherein the heavens being on fire shall be dissolved, and the elements shall melt with fervent heat ? Nevertheless we, according to his promise, look for new heavens and a new earth, wherein dwelleth righteousness. Wherefore, beloved, seeing that ye look for such things, be diligent that ye may be found of him in peace, without spot, and blameless."—II. *Peter*, iii : 10—14.

"The day of the Lord," is the gospel day, or judgment day, and was to come as a thief in the night, for the kingdom of God was not to come with observation, (*Luke*, xvii : 20,) but, like the thief, it was to steal upon them unseen. As it was in the overthrow of Sodom, when it rained fire upon the city from heaven, and destroyed them all, so was it to be at the destruction of Jerusalem, " Even thus shall it be in the day when the Son of man is revealed," (*Luke*, xvii : 30,) which was the day that he rained destruction and death upon the Jewish throne and kingdom, and established in their place the throne and kingdom of the everlasting gospel. For it is declared that at the destruction of Jerusalem, Two shall be in the field ; the one shall be taken, and the other left ; "Two women shall be grinding at the mill; the one shall be taken, and the other left. Watch therefore ; for ye know not what hour your Lord doth come. But know this, that if the good man of the house had known in what watch the thief would come, he would have watched, and would not have suffered his house to be broken up. Therefore be ye also ready : for in such an hour as ye think not the Son of man cometh." (*Matt.*, xxiv : 40—44.) This was the coming of the Son of man at the destruction of Jerusalem, and shows plainly that the day of the Lord, that was to come as a thief in the night, was the coming in of the gospel kingdom, at the end of the Jewish economy. The passing away of the heavens with a great noise was the passing away of the Jewish church and religion amid the lamentations of their nation. "And the elements shall melt with fervent heat." This was the burning up of their city, temple, and altar, and all the visible elements of their worship. " The earth also, and the works that are therein shall be burned up." This was their law of rites and ceremonies, their types and shadows, and all their outward signs and symbols, which were all of an earthly character, and were destroyed at the burning of their great city, being all terminated and fulfilled in the gospel of Christ. "Seeing then that all these things shall be dissolved, what manner of persons ought ye to be in all holy conversation and godliness, looking for and hasting unto the coming of the day of God." In this the apostle urges them to live in all holy conversation and godliness, to be ready for the coming of the day of God, which was the gospel day, and for which they were looking, and which was scarcely six years from them at that time ; and shows to all, clearly, that the apostles and disciples were all expecting the second coming of Christ, or they would not have been looking for him. "Wherein the heavens being on fire shall be dissolved." This was the Jewish religion with its covenant and economy, which was ended, or dissolved at the coming in of the gospel of Christ. "And the elements shall melt with fervent heat." This was the consuming of all the visible elements of the Hebrew religion, at the destruction of the temple and city of Jerusalem. "Nevertheless we, according to his promise, look for new heavens and a new earth, wherein dwelleth righteousness." The old heavens, that were destroyed, were the old covenant or Jewish religion. The new heavens and the new earth, is the new covenant or the religion of the Savior, established at the end of the Jewish church. "Wherefore, beloved, seeing that ye look for such things, be diligent, that ye may be found of him in peace, without spot and blameless." As they were looking for these things which were to accompany the coming of the Son of man, the apostle exhorts them to be diligent, that they might be found of him in peace, when he did come, or that he might find them at his second advent in peace, without spot and blameless. Thus showing that they were not only expecting the coming of the Son of God, but that they, everywhere, admonished the members of the churches to be prepared for the glorious event that was just at hand. And O, may we of this day, who live beneath the drapery of the gospel throne, enjoying all the blessings and benefits of the spiritual kingdom of our Lord and Savior, now established on earth, behold the beauty, love and power of his dominion, and by faith and obedience to his reign, become righteous citizens of his kingdom.

"Now we beseech you, brethren, by the coming of our Lord Jesus Christ, and by our gathering together unto him, That ye be not soon shaken in mind, or be troubled, neither by spirit, nor by word, nor by letter as from us, as that the day of Christ is at hand."—II. Thes., ii: 1—2.

As Christ's first coming was past, this of course was his second coming, and as the apostle urged the brethren, by the coming of our Lord Jesus Christ, and by their gathering together unto him, that they should not be shaken in mind, or troubled, neither by spirit nor word, nor by letter as from the apostles, as that the day of Christ was at hand, shows, beyond all doubt, that his second coming was certain and immediate, and that the church was not only looking for and expecting the Son of man to appear in his kingdom, but that they believed it near by, or the apostle would not have said that the day of Christ, or the gospel day, was at hand.

"And as he sat upon the mount of Olives, the disciples came unto him privately, saying, Tell us, when shall these things be? and what shall be the sign of thy coming, and of the end of the world?"—Matt., xxiv: 3.

The three great questions here asked by the disciples were all clearly answered by the Savior in this same chapter. The first question was, "When shall these things be?" that is, when shall the temple and Jerusalem be destroyed? The blessed Redeemer, after giving them the signs that should precede the fall and ruin of the holy city, tells them in the fifteenth and sixteenth verses that "When ye, therefore, shall see the abomination of desolation, spoken of by Daniel the prophet, stand in the holy place, (whoso readeth, let him understand,) Then let them which be in Judea flee into the mountains." The abomination of desolation was the Roman standards around Jerusalem, and when they, the Christians, beheld these, then they were to flee to the mountains, to avoid being destroyed in the overthrow of the temple and city, which shows that these things were to be in the lifetime of the disciples. The second question was, "And what shall be the sign of thy coming?" That is, the second coming of the Savior, in his spiritual kingdom, to establish the throne of his gospel and judgment on the earth. After giving the signs that were to precede his second coming, the Son of God, in the twenty-seventh and twenty-eighth verses, declared to them that "As the lightning cometh out of the east, and shineth even unto the west; so shall also the coming of the Son of Man be. For 'wheresoever the carcass is, there will the eagles be gathered together." The carcass was the destroyed city and nationality of the Jews, and the eagles were the standards of the Roman armies, gathered together on the ruins of the Hebrew empire; and the coming of the Son of Man like lightning was the bringing in of his gospel kingdom and the fulfiling of the types and shadows, the moment the Jewish religion and their nationality was destroyed or taken out of the way. The third and last question of the disciples was, "And of the end of the world?" or the end of the Jewish world, or the end of the Jewish age. The Savior, after giving all the signs preceding the end of the Jewish economy, told them in the thirty-fourth verse: "Verily, I say unto you, This generation shall not pass, till all these things be fulfilled." That is, the Jewish age, with all its glory, within the lifetime of that generation, should end forever and the gospel of Jehovah be established in its stead.

"Watch therefore; for ye know not what hour your Lord doth come."—*Matt.*, xxiv: 42.

This was spoken in reference to our Lord's coming in his kingdom at the destruction of Jerusalem. They were commanded to watch and be ready for the mighty event that was approaching; when mankind were to be resurrected out of the graves of trespass and sin, into the light and liberty of the gospel of Christ; the kingdom of Satan overthrown from the sovereignty of the world; the judgment and the gospel established on earth, and mankind brought unto nearness with God.

"And into whatever city ye enter, and they receive you, eat such things as are set before you. And heal the sick that are therein, and say unto them, The kingdom of God is come nigh unto you."—*Luke*, x: 8—9.

From this we learn that the Savior not only taught his disciples to heal the sick, and teach his gospel, but that they were to preach that the kingdom of God was nigh unto the people; that the day of the gospel and the judgment was nigh at hand.

"For whosoever shall be ashamed of me, and of my words, of him shall the Son of man be ashamed, when he shall come in his own glory, and in his Father's, and of the holy angels. But I tell you of a truth, there be some standing here which shall not taste of death till they see the kingdom of God."—*Luke*, ix: 26—27.

This shows us clearly that there were those then standing around the Savior, who would live to see the coming in of the kingdom of God. That they should not die until the gospel kingdom was established, and the way of salvation, the first resurrection, and the judgment, completed among men.

"And as they heard these things, he added and spake a parable, because he was nigh to Jerusalem, and because they thought that the kingdom of God should immediately appear."—*Luke*, xix: 11.

This Scripture, being in harmony with all others on the second coming of Christ, shows us that the disciples believed the doctrine in all its fulness, for they thought that the kingdom of God would immediately appear. But Christ, by the parable of the nobleman, explained that the gospel kingdom would not come until his enemies, the Jews, were destroyed.

"Joseph of Arimathea, an honorable councillor, which also waited for the kingdom of God, came, and went in boldly unto Pilate, and craved the body of Jesus."—*Mark*, xv: 43.

By this we learn that not only the disciples, but all the believers in Christ, embraced the doctrine of his second coming. That even this honorable councillor, who laid the body of Christ in his own new tomb, waited for the kingdom of God to appear on earth.

"For I know nothing by myself; yet am I not hereby justified: but he that judgeth me is the Lord. Therefore judge nothing before the time, until the Lord come, who both will bring to light the hidden things of darkness, and will make manifest the councils of the hearts: and then shall every man have praise of God."—I. *Cor.*, iv: 4—5.

The apostle "knew nothing by himself," that is, he was not conscious of any selfishness or dishonesty in himself, "Yet he was not thereby justified;" God could see many transgressions where he could see none. "For he that judgeth me is the Lord," not that is going to judge me away at the end of time, but judgeth me now, in the present tense. The judgment, like redemption, extended backward as well as forward, to all the children of our race. Although redemption did not take place until the Redeemer died on Calvary, yet its power extended back to Adam, as well as forward to the last-born child of man. And so, the judgment did not take place until the coming in of the gospel kingdom at the destruction of Jerusalem, yet its virtues extended back to the first family of our race, as well as forward to the last born. "Therefore judge nothing before the time, until the Lord come." This shows clearly that the apostle believed, and taught, that the second coming of Christ was near at hand. Indeed, it was scarcely twelve years from this admonition of the apostle, until the gospel day, which is the judgment day, was ushered in at the end of the Jewish economy. "Who will both bring to light the hidden things of darkness, and will manifest the council of the hearts: and then shall every man have praise of God," for all the deeds he has done well.

"Let your moderation be known unto all men. The Lord is at hand."—*Phil.*, iv : 5.

This admonition was given only about eight years before the second coming of our Lord, when he came in his spiritual kingdom, and established the throne of his judgment, and gospel, on earth, and shows how clearly and plainly the Savior and his disciples, taught the second coming of the Son of God being near at hand.

"For yet a little while, and he that shall come will come, and will not tarry."—*Heb.*, x : 37.

This was written to the Jewish Christians in order to comfort and strengthen them in the great doctrines of the gospel kingdom, which was near at hand, for this was written only about seven years before the second coming of Christ, when he destroyed the Hebrew nationality, ended the Jewish economy, established the first resurrection, subjected the kingdom of Satan, founded his own spiritual kingdom, and set up the throne of his judgment on earth. Well might the apostle say in that day; "For yet a little while, and he that shall come will come, and will not tarry."

"He which testifieth these things sayeth, Surely I come quickly: Amen. Even so, come, Lord Jesus."—*Rev.*, xxii : 20.

He which testified these things was the Lord Jesus Christ, who had everywhere told the world of his second coming: that it would be before that generation should pass away; that there were some standing there that would not die until they had seen him come; and then again, that he was near at hand; that he was even at the doors; that he would not tarry; and then he declares : "Surely I come quickly." That is, without doubt he would come immediately. "Amen ;" let it be done. "Even so, come, Lord Jesus," was the response of heaven, and it was done. Revelation was completed ; the Jewish church was ended ; the types and shadows were all fulfilled ; the Hebrew nationality, with its temple and covenant, passed away, and Jesus Christ, enthroned in the spiritual kingdom of his glorious gospel, descended to earth and resurrected our race out of the graves of original sin and death, vanquished Satan and established his spiritual dominion and judgment over the world of man.

"When the Son of man shall come in his glory, and all the holy angels with him, then shall he sit upon the throne of his glory : And before him shall be gathered all nations : and he shall separate them one from another, as a shepherd divideth his sheep from the goats. And he shall set the sheep on his right hand, but the goats on the left."—*Matt.*, xxv : 31—33.

This was the coming in of the gospel kingdom, so much spoken of by Christ and his apostles. "Coming in his glory," was the superiority of the descending spiritual kingdom of the gospel, over the temporal, earthly kingdom of the Jews. "And all the holy angels with him." These were the holy inhabitants of his heavenly kingdom that came with him in his glory. "Then shall he sit upon the throne of his glory." This is the spiritual throne of the gospel, and the judgment, established among men on earth. "And before him shall be gathered all nations." As the gospel kingdom embraces the world, with all its kingdoms, of course all nations are gathered before him, and every living being is now on trial at the bar of his gospel judgment, and will receive his sentence immediately after death, at the judgment seat of Christ. "And he shall separate them one from another, as a shepherd divideth the sheep from the goats." This separation is everywhere visible; it is not only seen between the heathen, and Christian nations of the Protestant world, but it is seen between the religious and irreligious communities, and still more plainly between the individual righteous and wicked. The righteous, who are represented by the sheep, are everywhere known by their gentle, harmless, kind and social disposition, while the wicked, who are represented by the goats, are just as clearly known by their proud, cruel and useless lives, so that the separation between the two is too plainly visible to be misunderstood. "And he shall set the sheep on his right hand, but the goats on his left." This is also just as evident, for the righteous are everywhere on the side of virtue, innocence and truth, which places them on the right side, and, of course, on the right hand of God. But the wicked, who are always on the side of wrong, are, of course, on the left hand of God. Thus might we go on unto the end of this chapter, but as we have explained it together with the twelfth chapter of Daniel and the twentieth chapter of Revelation, in our comment on the Scriptures of the first resurrection, we will not repeat it here, but merely say that this chapter, with all others on the subject of the judgment, so clearly demonstrates that the gospel day is the judgment day, that we are astonished that the teachers of Christianity should suffer the plain and simple doctrines of Christ, on the judgment, to lie buried beneath the rubbish of human creeds and councils, for fifteen hundred years, without a single effort to remove it from the debris of human systems, back to its primitive intention in the doctrines of Christ. O, that we could all realize that the gospel of Christ is spiritual, and that we are all spiritual beings; then we would be able to understand that the gospel day is the judgment day; that we are all in a state of probation or trial before the bar of God, while in life and time, and that immediately after death we shall appear before the judgment seat of Christ, in the spirit world, where we will receive the final verdict, according to the deeds done while we were in the body. If good has been the prevailing intention and action of our life on earth, we shall receive a crown of glory and go away into everlasting joy in the paradise of God, where we shall rise from glory to glory while eternity itself shall endure.' But if, on the other hand, evil has been the prevailing intention and action of our life on earth, we shall receive the sentence that assigns us to hell, where sorrow and dispair will be ours while the endless ages of eternity shall roll along.

Having noticed all the Scriptures that have a direct bearing on the subject of the judgment, and having shown, as we believe, beyond successful contradiction, that there is no evidence in the word of God to sustain the idea of a general judgment, we now proceed to notice a few reasons in support of the judgment established by Christ, and against the idea of a general judgment, as taught by men.

If there be no judgment until the end of time, then only a portion of the righteous would receive equal and impartial justice, while the other portion would receive injustice and wrong. For some of the righteous would be judged immediately after death, while others would have to wait for thousands of years to have their case decided. For instance, those who would die the day before the judgment, would be judged immediately, while righteous Abel, Noah, Deborah, and Stephen, with all the righteous of their day, would have to wait thousands of years before their case could be heard, which would show a preference of one portion of the righteous over the other, which would not be allowed, even in the earthly courts of mankind; for a speedy trial by jury is the highest prerogative of human jurisprudence. And yet this tenet of men would palm, on God, a doctrine that is nowhere allowed among civilized beings; while, on the other hand, the judgment, as taught by Christ, is plain and simple, and easily understood. "Now is the judgment of this world." All are being judged as they pass along, and at death receive the final verdict, and are sent to their eternal abode, to heaven or hell, according to the actions of their lives.

Again, if the judgment does not take place until the end of the world, then one portion of the wicked would be made to suffer more than the other. For they who die the day before the judgment will immediately be judged and sent into the world of woe and misery, forever, while the wicked Antediluvians, the sinners of Sodom and Gomorrah, and others, have had their judgment delayed for thousands of years before entering their final place of torment and woe; thus exempting the wicked Ancients for scores of centuries from judgment and condemnation, while the wicked Moderns are judged, and condemned, and sent to hell, without the exemption of a day; so that one portion of the wicked, though equal in sin and crime, have preference over the other, which is not only contrary to all human reason, but the word of God itself; while the doctrine of the blessed Savior shows that the children of men are judged in this life, and receive their sentence at death, according to the deeds done in the body.

Then, again, if there is no judgment until the last day of time, the righteous do not go to heaven at death, for none can get there without passing the ordeal of the judgment, as all must be judged worthy before being admitted into the heaven of eternal life. And if there be no judgment until the end of time, the righteous dead must, therefore, have some middle state or place, where they remain until the judgment; which is not only contrary to both Scripture and reason, but is in direct opposition to the hopes and expectations of every sincere and candid Christian. While the plain, simple doctrine of the Scriptures shows that every accountable human being is judged in life and time, and that the righteous receive the verdict at death, and enter at once into Paradise, the first mansion in the heaven of God, where they will rise from glory to glory while eternity endures.

And again, if there be no judgment until the end of time, then the wicked do not go to hell at death, for none can be punished until they are condemned, and none can be condemned until they are tried, judged and found guilty. But if there be no judgment until the end of the world, then the wicked dead must have some middle state or place, where they will remain until the judgment; which is not only opposed to sound reason, but is contrary to the doctrine of God's word concerning the future state of the wicked; while the teachings of Christ and his disciples show clearly that every human being, as soon as they come to the years of accountability, is judged according to his actions, as they are performed along the journey of life, and that the wicked receive the sentence of the judgment at death, and enter at once into hell, where they are punished forever.

Again, if there is no judgment until the end of the world, and no intermediate place, or middle state, for the righteous between death and the judgment, then the righteous, when they die, would go immediately to heaven and remain there until the end of the world; when they would all be brought out of heaven to the judgment, where they would be judged and then sent back again to heaven, just as they were before the judgment. So that when they die they go to heaven, and stay there until the judgment, are then brought out of heaven, judged and sent back again to heaven; which is not only contrary to the common sense of mankind, but is in direct opposition to the Scriptures of Divine Truth. While, on the other hand, the gospel of the Redeemer distinctly teaches that he came into the world for judgment; that all mankind are now on trial before the judgment throne of the gospel kingdom, and, at death, will be sentenced according to their works—the righteous to heaven and the wicked to hell.

And again, if the judgment does not take place until the

end of time, and there is no middle place or state for the wicked to abide in between death and the judgment, then the wicked, when they die, would go immediately to hell, and would remain there until the end of time, when they would all be brought out of hell to the judgment, where they would be judged and sent back again to hell, just as they were before the judgment; so that when the wicked die, they go immediately to hell and are kept there until the judgment, then brought out of hell, judged and sent back again to hell, which is not only unreasonable in itself, but stands opposed to all the teachings of Christ; while the doctrines of the gospel fully demonstrate that the gospel day is the judgment day, and that the judgment is now going on. That every action a man does, he feels the decision of the judgment within himself, whether it is right or wrong, unless he has become so wicked that his conscience has become seared, and there remains nothing but a fearful looking for of judgment after death.

Again, the existence of a general judgment at the end of time would disturb the harmony of heaven, and bring mourning and anguish upon all the sainted millions of the redeemed. For the doctrine of a general judgment teaches that all the holy and happy populations of the saved in glory will appear on the right hand of the Son of God, and that all the sumless numbers of the lost in hell will appear on his left hand, face to face with the heavenly hosts. There the righteous husband will see his lost and ruined wife, the companion of his life on earth, in the agony of woe, stretching out her hands to him for help, which would not only fill his righteous soul with grief, and destroy his happiness in heaven, but he would feel like flying to her relief, and sharing, with her, her awful destiny of misery, rather than endure such a dreadful parting. Surely the blessed Savior has never ordained that any of his righteous children should pass through such an ordeal of anguish and woe, after being in heaven for hundreds of years. No, thank heaven, there is no such doctrine taught in the gospel of God. "The Judge standeth at the door" of every man's heart, and judges every one of us as we pass through life, and at death we will receive the verdict according to the deeds done in the body, and be assigned to heaven or hell, never to be brought out any more.

There, too, according to the doctrines of a general judgment, the righteous wife will behold her lost and undone husband, the companion of her life in time and earth, enveloped in flame and staggering with despair, reaching forth his imploring hands, as he calls to her for aid, in moans of woe that thrill her soul with pain, and ruins all her heavenly joy, until her stricken spirit, filled with woful grief, would gladly hasten to his aid, or share his doom, rather than suffer such a dread farewell with him she loved so tenderly on earth. Surely, our Heavenly Father will never bring any of his children from glory, to endure such scenes of agony and woe, after being admitted to the kingdom of immortality and eternal life. O, no; he has prepared his throne for judgment on earth, where every one is judged as he passes along, and receives his final award at death. The righteous, crowned with glory, join the ransomed hosts in the paradise of God, where they increase in wisdom, happiness and glory forever, while the wicked pass away into everlasting woe, to be known or remembered, by their kindred in heaven, no more forever.

And there, too, according to the doctrines of a general judgment, righteous and holy parents will come out from the realms of happiness and angelic glory, to meet their lost and ruined children on the left hand of God, reaching out their blazing hands, and crying in shrieks of fiery pain to them for help, until their screams of torment pierce their parents' hearts with pangs of grief that wither all their joys of heaven, and make them shrink and shudder, until their anguish-burdened souls would fain embrace the agonizing ghosts of their ruined offspring and share their woe, rather than endure such frightful separation with those they loved so dearly on earth. It cannot be that our holy and blessed Savior would destroy the happiness of his redeemed and holy children by bringing them out of heaven to look upon the rage of devils, the contortions of the damned, and to listen to the screams and yells of their undone kindred. O, no; he has provided a perfect and righteous judgment, by which all are judged in life and time and sentenced at death. The righteous being called to their home in heaven, and the wicked sent to their home in hell, never to meet again while eternity endures.

There, too, according to the human doctrines of a general judgment, happy and righteous children, from the courts of glory, will be doomed to see the shrieking ghosts of their lost parents, coming up from the regions of the damned, and taking their stand among the burning hosts of death, on the left of the throne of God, to hear the Judge remand them to hell. There, too, according to this awful doctrine, will righteous brothers from the kingdom of heaven meet the lost and distorted souls of once lovely sisters, coming up from the chambers of woe, writhing in anguish and livid with horror, imploring their aid. And there will holy and righteous sisters, just from the mansions of bliss, behold the frightful forms of their doomed and ruined brothers, from the pavements of hell, distorted with remorse and raging with torment, taking their place on the left of the Judge, to hear their doom and depart to the same hell from which they came. And so, with neighbors, kindreds and tongues, according to this dreadful doctrine, all the hosts of heaven will stand face to face with all the hosts of hell. The immortal throngs of glory, millions of whom have rejoiced around the throne of God for thousands of years, will be called out of heaven to meet with howling devils and damned ghosts, in judgment, and to see their husbands, wives and children, parents, friends and neighbors, in blazing death, hurled headlong down the molten cliffs of dark damnation, where screaming winds and billowy tempests rage and roar through all the caverns of the lost, and ruined souls forever plunge and shriek amid the blazing waves of death, without a moment's rest, within the lake of hell. O, where is the righteous soul that could look upon such a scene without suffering all the pangs that grief and anguish can inflict? And yet, we are told that God will bring all the sainted millions out of heaven to witness this dreadful exhibition of a general judgment, and that, for the sole purpose of showing to the world, that his judgment is just, which is a doctrine that impeaches the justice and rectitude of the Supreme Judge of the world, in that it presumes that God cannot judge the world without the general consent of mankind to its correctness, or without the world of mankind standing by, to see that it is justly done; as though the eternal God, who made the world, created our race, and beholds every thought, word and action of the heart, was not able to decide the destiny of mortals without the approbation of mankind, who are but finite beings, and know not what is right or wrong, only as they receive the knowledge from God. But we rejoice and are happy to know, by the word, that the Savior of the world, at the setting up of his gospel kingdom on earth, hath established the throne of his judgment, by which all the children of men are judged according to their actions, as they pass down the stream of life and time, and that the decision is given at death that assigns them to their eternal destiny. And this gospel judgment, like the gospel Redemption, extended backward, up to the first family of man, as well as forward, down to the last child born ; so that all mankind have had the benefit of the judgment, as well as of the benefit of the redemption, from the beginning of our race, down to the present time, and will have, as long as time endures.

And if there be no day of judgment until the end of time, it would be impossible to judge the whole race of mankind in a single day, and though that day should be a thousand years, it would still be impossible, since every thought, word and action must be judged. And as it sometimes consumes days in the trial and judgment of one man, for a single crime, in the courts of earth, how long would it take to try and judge every thought, word and action of a whole human life, guilty of thousands of sins, and then think of the countless millions of mankind to be judged in this way, and we will see that a thousand centuries will be far too short for the day of judgment? And yet the righteous must stand and listen to the screams of their kindred, the yells of devils, and the shrieks of the damned, and look upon their anguish during the continuance of the judgment, for more than a thousand centuries. O, who can endure the thought that the righteous must suffer this awful scene of sorrow and agony for the interval of ages? And yet this dreadful conclusion cannot be avoided, if there be a day of general judgment, when all mankind will be tried and judged for every thought, word and action. Nor will it do to say that God will condense the judgment so as to alter or change the laws or being of mankind, for that would make them different beings from what they were on earth, and they could not be judged as the same beings. To make them anything more, or anything less than human beings, at the judgment, would be to destroy their identity, and consequently take away their accountability, so that mankind must be judged according to the laws of mind, as well as the laws of God, without any change in the laws of intellect or being. Hence, the day of general judgment, if mankind are judged for all the actions of their lives, must continue for thousands of ages, and the sainted millions of glory will be forced to stand face to face with the wicked millions of the lost, during that dreadful period, or until the judgment is consummated. But, thanks be God, there is no such word as general judgment in the Holy Scriptures, but, on the contrary, our blessed Redeemer hath brought "forth judgment to the Gentiles," (*Isa.*, xlii : 1,) and executeth "judgment and justice in the earth."—(*Jer.*, xxiii : 5.) He was not to fail till he had "set judgment in the earth."—(*Isa.*, xlii : 4.) "Every morning doth he bring his judgment to light, he faileth not."—(*Zeph.*, iii : 5.) For "According to their doings I judged them."—(*Eze.*, xxxvi : 19.) " Verily he is a God that judgeth in the earth."—(*Psa.*, lviii : 11.) "He shall minister judgment to the people in uprightness."—(*Psa.*, ix : 8.) For "the Lord is known by the judgment which he executeth."—(*Psa.*, ix : 16.) "Every man's judgment cometh from the Lord."—(*Prov.*, xxix : 26.) "And a wise man's heart discerneth both time and judgment."—(*Eccl.*, viii : 5.) "And he shall shew judgment to the Gentiles."—(*Matt.*, xii : 18.) "For judgment I am come into the world."—(*John,* ix : 39.) "He that is spiritual judgeth all things."—(I. *Cor.*, ii : 15.) "And he shall execute judgment and righteousness in the land."—(*Jer.*, xxxiii : 15.) For "he that judgeth me is the Lord."—(I. *Cor.*, iv : 4.) "Now is the judgment of this world."—(*John,* xii : 31.) Thus might we go on adding Scripture to Scripture until the reader would become weary of their number, but we think the above short texts enough to satisfy every candid searcher after truth, that the judgment is a present judgment, and that it is now going on among men in the earth, under the gospel reign of Christ, in his spiritual kingdom, who is the Supreme Judge, of the world. For he " was ordained of God to be the judge of quick and dead."—(*Acts,* x : 42.) The quick are the living on earth, and the dead are those who have ceased to live on earth, so that he is the judge of the living and the dead ; that is, he judges the living as they journey along toward eternity, and as soon as they enter there they receive their final judgment, which fixes their destiny forever. "The Lord Jesus Christ, who shall judge the quick and the dead at his appearing and his kingdom."—(II. *Tim.*, iv : 1.) His appearing and his kingdom was when he came in his gospel kingdom, at the end of the Jewish kingdom, and established his judgment of the quick and the dead, or of the living and the dead. The living are all judged for every act they do in life, whether good or bad, and every accountable being knows this to be the case, for they feel either condemned or cleared, according to the acts

ʻthey do, as soon as they are done, and this proves to all that God is everywhere judging the living. And that he will judge them to their final destiny at death, must be evident to all, so that it may be truly said he is the Judge of the quick and the dead. "Who shall give an account to him that is ready to judge the quick and the dead."—(I. *Peter*, iv : 5.) This was written only a little while before the second coming of Christ to establish his gospel judgment, so that he was ready to judge the quick and the dead. That is, to judge the living in life and time, and the dead immediately after death. The living are judged according to their actions, as they pass along through life, and immediately after death they receive the decision or verdict of that judgment, in the spirit world, where the righteous will receive a crown of life and enter at once into everlasting glory, in the Paradise of God, but the wicked shall be sentenced to everlasting condemnation, from the presence of the Lord, and the glory of his power. O, may the spirit of the living God ever bless and guide every reader of these pages, that when they appear at death, before the judgment seat of Christ, they may receive a crown of righteousness and be saved forever.

Having briefly elucidated, both from Scripture and reason, that every living, intelligent human being is now on trial or probation before the bar of God, that they are judged for all the deeds done in the body as they pass along through life, and that they receive the final judgment, or award, immediately after death, when the righteous receive their crowns of immortal glory and enter at once into the mansions of eternal life, to go out no more forever, and when the wicked receive the burning curse of their endless destiny, and are driven away to the remorseful regions of an undone eternity, to be punished forevermore.

We will now, in conclusion, view the sum of human destiny as awarded by Jehovah, the Supreme Judge of the universe, according to the records of Inspiration. And O, may the thoughts of our hearts be inspired by the spirit of God, while we indite the truths of Divinity, and rehearse the destiny of man.

The good man, in his travel to eternity, becomes at once assured that judgment has come upon all men, as every action in his march of life harmonizes with the disclosures of Revelation and tells him that the judgment is here, and now with him ; because every deed of his being, in the journey of his existence, is either approved or condemned as they transpire. If he does an evil action, he feels at once the power of the judgment condemning him, and if he does a good action, he feels at once the power of the judgment approving him, by which he feels and knows that God is ever with him, which blessed and holy truth, the doctrine of a general judgment denies to man, by putting off the judgment until the end of the world ; while the truths of a present and eternal judgment show that God is ever with the children of our race, approving or condemning the actions of men, and proving, to a demonstration, what our blessed Savior affirmed : that, " For judgment I am come into the world ;" that " Now is the judgment of this world ;" and that, "As I hear I judge and my judgment is just;" which harmonize with all the other Scripture upon this great axiom of eternal truth, and show that all the living generations of mankind are now on a state of trial before God, and must soon stand before the judgment seat of Christ, in the Spirit world, where they will receive the verdict of weal or woe, according to their righteous or wicked lives.

Having thus attested his own immortality by the presence of God in the judgment, the good man advances in the march of his being and nears the margin of eternity ; earth and time begin to fade in the azure of distance; like the far off mountains to the departing mariner, they vanish into air and are lost in the sunset glory of the starry world. Then it is that he beholds, for the first time, the brilliant shore of the summer land, as it flashes the splendors of its magnificence upon his enraptured vision. He sees the blooming groves and bending trees of paradise, in brightening distance, nod their fruitful boughs in waves of purple silver, throwing their gorgeous drapery of living emerald over the pavilions of the blest, while from the radiant skies of hallowed glory, come the sweet hosannas of eternal life, rolling in lovely cadence on all the paths of sound, and pealing through all the camps and courts of heaven, the anthems of redemption and the welcome of the saved. Nearing still the shores of the immortal world, he at last beholds the judgment seat of Christ, the splendors of whose throne cast the effulgence of an eternal sunrise on all the realms that emboss the canopy of God ; while round him roll in steady radiance the powers of Omnipotence, that everywhere wield the energies and control the fortunes of the universe.

Standing at last upon the edge of time, he gazes for a moment upon the margin of the spirit world, then drops his tabernacle of corruption, and appears before the Almighty Arbiter of destiny, the Supreme Judge of men and angels, whose awful glory flashes the light of Godhead through all the vast and mighty wilderness of worlds that begirt the habitation of his throne. Robed in vesture blazing with the brilliance of Divinity, his face brighter than the light of a thousand suns, and with a smile that thrills his pavilion with the hallelujahs of eternity, he bids the happy soul come near, pronounces the verdict of the judgment of salvation, and with his own right hand invests him with garments of celestial splendor, and with his left hand crowns him with the righteous diadem of eternal beauty, and with the kiss of endless love he introduces him to the waiting angels, who, swift as the lightning's flight, bear him to the Paradise of God, where he joins the sainted millions of happy immortals, and begins his enraptured march of eternal glory. Introduced to prophets, priests and sages, and to the redeemed of our wise and holy ancestry, to angel friends and kindred, all radiant with beauty and glittering with glory, they walk the heavens in roseate youth, viewing the wonders of Omnipotence, as they are everywhere strewn through the mansions of eternity, in bowers of rapture and banquets of love, until the roll of the hosannas of Jehovah, the harmonious pealing of the anthems of redemption fill every mind with immortal enchantment and pour a heavenly beatitude over all the fields and temples of Paradise, where the mantling beauty of its splendors becomes more entrancing than the bloom and melody of a thousand springs. And yet this is but one step in the journey of our illustrious destiny; for we shall go in to come out no more forever. Our march shall be onward and upward throughout eternity. From clime to clime, along with all the adoring millions of Jehovah, the happy soul shall rise to higher worlds of purer joy, to brighter realms of the infinite glory that are everywhere throughout the immensity of God's domain. And when we shall have traveled with all the blooming and happy children of Immanuel, for more than a million of ages, and visited a thousand mansions of ecstatic blessedness in the universe of the Almighty, which is but our Father's House, we will scarce have crossed the frontiers of the Creator's eternal kingdom, or begun the march of our glorious destiny. O, then, who would not be a follower of Christ, that they might know him in the judgment, while they live on earth, and after death receive, from him, a crown of righteousness that shall give them immortality and eternal life through all the ages of a blessed and happy eternity?

But, with a feeling of sadness, we turn to the sinner and view him as he passes the ordeal of the judgment, according to the gospel of Revelation. The wicked man, in his journey to eternity, is also forced to acknowledge "that judgment has come upon all men;" because every action. of his life accords with Revelation, and tells him that the judgment is here on earth; for every deed he performs is either approved or condemned by the Judge, the moment it is done. If he does a good action, he feels the power of the judgment approving him, but if he does an evil action, he also feels the power of the judgment condemning him, (unless his conscience has become seared as with a hot iron;) which clearly proves that all mankind are now on trial before God, and are being judged for the deeds done in the body, and that all must appear at death before the judgment seat of Christ, where they will receive the verdict of the judgment, which will consign them to heaven or to hell, according to their righteous or wicked lives on earth. Having thus attested his own immortality by the presence of God in the judgment, the wicked man advances in the travel of his existence, and nears the shores of eternity. Earth and time begin to fade in the darkening distance. All his hopes and pleasures now are vanishing; the gloom of an endless night seems to be settling about him. Then it is that he awakes to his dreadful situation, and starts aghast at the awful destiny before him. Nearing, still, the margin of the spirit world, he stands at last upon the farther shore of time and looks with horror on the cold and turbid stream of death, that, like a midnight Jordan, rolls in putrefaction at his feet. Clinging to its house of flesh and blood, the awe-struck soul raves round the walls and calls for help; but O, there's none. It weeps, and groans, and flies to every avenue for aid, till forced upon the last terrific cliff, in wild remorse and fierce despair, the horror-stricken spirit takes its awful flight and stands in dread dismay before the judgment seat of Christ. Here the daylight of eternity awakes the slumber of his crimes, until the shuddering offender reels beneath his guilt, that, like an eternal Sinai, piles to heaven and will crush him down to everlasting death. Stung with dread remorse, more awful than the scorpion's pang, and filled with all the horrors of despair, he hears the just and holy Judge pronounce the dreadful verdict of his endless doom. No stroke of the destroying angel was ever half so terrible as the uplifted arm of the avenging Godhead, when, by the immutable laws of the judgment, he consigns the ruined soul to its own chosen home of agony, in the ghostly realms of endless death. At once he sinks, and quick as thought can flash or mind can soar, he passes to the regions of the damned, where is only anguish, eternal, fixed and vast. Beyond this, no prayer is ever heard, no crime forgiven, or pardon found. Despair becomes the only pulse that throbs with life, and sighs and groans the only happiness the undone soul can know through all the unresting ages of agony and remorse. O, what are all the deaths of fever, flame and flood, compared with the death of that soul whose dying never ends? The fate of a thousand battles fought and lost; the march of pestilence, shedding plagues and curses from its blazing front on pallid millions; the wrath and ruin of storm and earthquake, leaving only wreck and desert in their track; what are these, compared to the pangs and throes of the lost soul, writhing in eternal death, shut up in the wilderness of hell, along with raging devils, furious fiends and cursed ghosts that everywhere people the dungeons of the damned? Spurned of heaven, forgotten by saints and abhorred of God, the condemned soul, with sobs of anguish and remorse, forever walks the desert of his black and gloomy orb, and wails the dirge of his own destruction with all the outcasts of eternity, where the cry of anguished millions, the shriek of fiends, the scream of devils and the roar of hell's damnation shall howl his doom while eternity shall roll its centuries on.

And yet the sons and daughters of men will heedlessly march through all the prayers and tears of friends; over all the songs and sermons of the church; through all the calls and warnings of the Spirit, and over all the barriers of the gospel of Christ, as though they would take eternal woe by storm, and rush on without a solitary preparation for the awful verdict of the judgment, that must sooner or later consign them to the horrors of the undone eternity they have so wilfully chosen.

O, may the Spirit of God inspire every reader to embrace the offers of salvation, that they all may share the glories of eternal redemption, and at last be filled and pavilioned around the throne of God in the heaven of heavens.

www.ingramcontent.com/pod-product-compliance
Lightning Source LLC
Chambersburg PA
CBHW031242260626
47169CB00007B/2417